FIRE

WILD FIRE

Edited by Nice girl, Naughty edits

Cover by Timeless Designs

1

FRANKIE

"Well, that's just great."

Scrunching up my nose, my angry glare flicked between my hand and kitchen bench. Or more specifically, the sticky white stuff covering both.

With a shake of my head, I muttered, "Who knew such a tiny hole could produce such a big mess. I mean, really." Still shaking my head, I swiped my clean index finger through the gloop on the bench before sticking said finger into my mouth. "Mmm, at least it tastes good."

Actually, it tasted better than good. It might have even been the best batch of elderflower frosting I'd made. And now no one was going to get to taste it.

Giving the mess one last longing look, I spun around to wash my hands.

I'd made it three steps when my dress's hidden pocket started buzzing obnoxiously. My poor heart almost gave out. Because I was incapable of thinking through the wild thundering behind my ribs, I smacked my dirty palm against my chest.

Slowly removing my hand, I eyed the white stain on my right boob before throwing my head back and shooting daggers at the ceiling. "Are you freaking kidding me right now?"

In all honesty, I probably should have known better than to try to get in a little baking two hours before I had to meet my date. I'd just been so damn inspired to try out the new recipe I'd come up with.

Pear muffins with a generous amount of frosting squeezed into the center.

It would've been so perfect with an elderflower gin cocktail.

What wasn't perfect was my little black dress with a palm-sized smudge on it.

The stupid buzzing finally died down long enough for me to start walking again. My relief was short-lived because I only made it a few steps before the thing started up yet again.

Muttering a few very unladylike curses under my breath, I fished out my phone to see my BFF's name flashing in big bold letters. With a quick flick of my thumb, I swiped the green button and held the device against my ear. "This better be good, Maddie-Cakes. I just made my boob sticky, and it's all your fault."

There were a few seconds of silence before, "Where are you?" her tone was serious, too serious. No, not serious, scared. My friend sounded scared.

"At the bakery, why?"

A shaky breath filtered through the line. "Oh, no. Frankie, please get out of there. Right now."

"What? Why?" I could hear her pacing through the phone. "Maddie, what's going on?"

"Adam just called. Mr. Hamilton's shop caught fire and they're struggling to put it out. He's worried because the buildings are old and so close together that the fire will spread too fast." Another shaky breath reached my ears. "Frankie, please get out of there. Sugar Booger is four shops away from the dry cleaner."

Maddie sounded so scared, and that made me scared too. "I'm going."

"Okay, good. Call me when you're home so I'll know you're safe."

"Promise."

I shoved my phone back into my pocket with every intention of turning around and marching my butt out of the bakery. That is, until I saw the muffins sitting pretty on the bench. The same bench still covered in frosting from when the piping bag's seam gave out.

I couldn't leave my kitchen like that.

Moving as fast as I could, I snatched a rag and cleaner from the sink and tidied up my workspace. The pungent smell of smoke hit my nostrils as I packed the muffins in an airtight container.

Shit, that was fast.

Panic clawed at my throat, and I walked as fast as my feet would allow. All I needed was to get the muffins to the storeroom and then get the hell out of there. I should've known better because all signs pointed to it not being my day.

In my hurried state, I kicked the stopper holding the door open. Realizing instantly what I did, I spun around, but the door had already clicked shut.

"No, no, no."

My heart flatlined for a nanosecond before it slammed against my ribs like a wild beast trying to make an escape. The walls started shifting, steadily closing in on me. This couldn't be happening.

One hand reached for the handle while the other furiously rubbed at my neck, desperately trying to get air to my lungs.

I needed to breathe. If only the damn door would open, and the walls would stop moving. My lips parted to call for help. Only no sound came. Nothing but the deafening thumps of my heart.

I tried the handle again, but whatever I did made my world spin. Around and around until up was down and right was left. My head connected with something hard causing cold sensations to travel along my skin.

My lids felt heavy and keeping them open was near impossible. Maybe I had time to close my eyes, just for a few minutes, until the world stopped going around and around.

I let out a breath, allowing my body to give in to the tiredness. It was so calm and peaceful until I was viciously pulled from my state of bliss.

My eyes flew open, my entire body shaking as I furiously coughed up fire from my lungs. There were people—an EMT and a firefighter—in front of me, desperately trying to get a mask to my face, but all I could see was the smoke billowing out of the building.

My building.

No. Oh, please no.

I needed to get inside, to save what was left of my bakery. In one quick move, I jumped up and shoved at the people before running to the entrance of Sugar Booger. I didn't make it very far when a strong arm snaked around my waist and yanked my back against a wall of hard muscles.

"You can't go in there."

The moment he spoke, every muscle in my body tensed. Because it might've been ten years, but I'd never forgotten that voice. It was one I both longed to hear and loathed at the same time.

Gage freaking Calloway.

I had no idea how I managed it, but I spun around and poked him in the chest. "You can't tell me what to do." Well, he probably could.

He stood stock-still for a few long seconds, and because he was still wearing his gear, I had no idea what his face was doing behind that mask. That was until he whipped the thing off.

One look at his face and my lungs collapsed in one big whoosh, leaving me with another coughing fit that had nothing to do with the smoke I'd inhaled. Hair wet and disheveled. Face sweaty and covered in soot. And yet, he was still the most beautiful man in my world.

My fingers tingled, remembering the feel of his whiskers beneath my touch. The way he held me. The words he'd whispered in my ear that night.

No.

Nope.

There was no way in hell I was going there. Not going to happen. Because as far as I was concerned, that night I offered up my v-card didn't exist anymore.

"You have to go to the hospital to get checked out," he said. "We don't know how much smoke got into your lungs while you were passed out in the storeroom." He took a step forward and reached for me. "Come on."

The chaos behind me reached new heights. Although I couldn't make out what they were saying, I could hear the other firefighters yell out orders at each other. Swallowing hard, my gaze traveled over Gage's shoulder to where more

EMTs were seeing to the people who'd been pulled out of the buildings.

Gosh, what a mess this night had turned into.

I felt a little buzz zip over my skin again and I knew it had nothing to do with adrenaline and everything with the man before. I turned my attention back to him. Grinning like a damn idiot, he was still holding out his hand for me.

I smacked it away. "I can walk by myself, thank you." To prove it, I lifted my chin and sauntered back to the open ambulance. I might've put an extra sway in my hips too. The EMT who tried to give me oxygen earlier helped me into the back and onto the waiting gurney.

I'd never admit it out loud while Gage was within earshot, but my chest did feel as if the gates of hell had opened and spilled out into my lungs. Getting it checked out was certainly the best course of action.

Laying back, I closed my eyes and waited for the ambulance to start moving. I could hear Gage and the EMT talk about something, but their voices were too muffled for me to make out.

A few seconds later, the vehicle shook as someone climbed in, followed by the doors slamming shut.

Eyes still closed, I asked, "Are we off?"

"We sure are."

My eyes flew open as I jerked into a seated position to find Gage hovering over my gurney. I gave him my best piss-off glare. "What the hell are you doing?"

Slowly, he inched closer. One corner of his mouth hitched up, making his stupid dimple pop. Oh, how wonderful it would've been to smack that smirk off his annoyingly sexy face. I wanted to do it so badly. Almost as much as I wanted him to stop leaning forward.

But of course, he didn't stop. Not until he was right up in my space, green eyes piercing into mine. "I just saved your life, Baker. You can say thank you now."

I didn't think it was possible, but I narrowed my eyes even more. Lifting my hand, I gave his cheek two taps before shoving my middle finger in the space between us. "There's your thank you, asshole."

Gage's eyes flicked to my finger before locking onto mine again. He studied me long and hard, making my skin prickle with unwanted awareness. Awareness that dissolved the instant he threw his head back and laughed.

"Still as feisty as I remember."

Not giving two shits that I was flipping him off, he patted the spot above my knee twice before parking his ass and leaning back against the inside of the ambulance.

As we steadily began to move, I knew two things for certain:

I was going to be so late for my date.

Gage Calloway needed to stay as far away from me as humanly possible

2

GAGE

How long can I hold my breath before I pass out?

That wasn't the only question floating around in my head as the ambulance made its way to the hospital, but it was the most pressing one. Because with every drag of air I sucked in, I took all things Frankie into my system.

Not that she hadn't been there for the better part of ten years.

But this, having her so close and yet so far away had to be the worst form of torture I could I think of. Especially when the feel of her was still branded into my skin. When my fingers burned with the need to brush along her skin or tangle in those inky tresses.

Shit, I'd been wanting to do that for far longer than I would ever admit. Mostly because her brother, who happened to be my best friend, might not take kindly to the obscene amount of illicit thoughts I'd had about his baby sister over the years.

Or that I'd taken her innocence before running like the hounds of hell were giving chase.

Yeah, I had no doubts he wouldn't be too happy about it and no amount of explaining on my part would change that. It didn't matter that Frankie had been the only woman to ever get under my skin or that she was the one who featured in every single one of my fever dreams.

Or that my heart had found a new rhythm the instant I'd seen her passed out on her storeroom floor. It didn't matter that my blood turned to lava or that every nerve ending in my body came alive when I scooped her up and carried her out of the building.

It didn't matter because I chose to run away from the one person who had the ability to set my soul on fire.

It had been one of my biggest regrets and the moment I'd made the decision to come back to Clearwater Bay, that was the one thing I wanted to set right. Only I wasn't prepared for the impact of seeing her again, and I definitely wasn't prepared for the level of anger she so clearly still had toward me.

"I don't understand why you're here."

I bit my cheek to stop myself from grinning. Even pissed off, her husky voice sounded sexy as sin. *What would my name on her tongue sound like now that she's older?*

"Seriously? You're just going to sit there and ignore me?" Her words came out in a huff. I almost gave in and opened my eyes just to see the exasperation on her pretty little face. "Typical. So damn typical."

I could easily picture those icy blue eyes glaring daggers at me. In fact, I was certain I felt the weight of her stare all the way to my toes. Still, I didn't give in. One part, because I knew I was getting her good and worked up and the other, because I was terrified I might just take her face in my hands and kiss her into silence.

"Hey! Shit for brains, I'm talking to you!"

I had to cover my mouth with my hand because, shit, I was losing the damn battle with my grin. As long as she thought her words had no effect on me, I had the upper hand.

And where Frankie Baker was concerned, I always needed the upper hand.

"I can't believe—"

The rest of her sentence died on her tongue when the ambulance suddenly came to a stop and the back doors swung open a moment later. Justin, the unfortunate EMT, barely had time to step inside before Frankie was off again.

"I'm no legal expert but I am positive he doesn't need to be in here with me. In fact, I think I am well within my rights to ask you to throw his ass to the curb."

Wide-eyed, Justin aimed his frown my way. "I…uh…"

If I wasn't feeling bad for the poor kid stumbling over his words, I would have kept my ass parked right where I was just to rile Frankie up some more. Because as damn sad as it sounded, this was the most fun I'd had in a long time.

Being the only parent to an almost teenager meant my days were filled with stress on top of some more stress. Even more so now that I had finally decided to chase after a dream I'd thought I'd buried a long time ago.

"Uhm, hello," Frankie's voice sounded.

This time, though. I did look her way and holy shit, I wasn't prepared. Big blue eyes—albeit filled with hate—stared straight at me, burning a hot path to the very bottom of my soul. Her nose—the very same one I'd kissed countless times in my dreams— scrunched up with disgust. And those lips I knew were gorgeous and plump, pressed into a thin, tight line.

And still, my damn dick stirred. How damn, ironic. The first woman to get me hard in who knew how long just happened to be her. But in all fairness, my dick had always had a soft—or was that hard—spot for Frankie Baker.

"Are you deaf or just dumb?" she barked out. "This lovely young fella said you can go." She pushed herself into a seated position, the action causing the buttons of her dress to gape, naturally drawing my eyes to her chest.

My palms tingled; I still remembered the feel of—

"Oh, for shit's sake, Gage. Get out!"

There was something very wrong with me. She was being downright rude, and here I was conjuring up a hundred different ways to shut her up—all of them ending with either my mouth on hers or her lips wrapped around me.

Thank heavens for thick gear or I might have found myself in awkward position when I pushed to my feet. Instead of heading out, like she so clearly wanted, I twisted my body and leaned toward her.

An excited thrill danced down my spine at her sharp intake of breath and her widening eyes. When I was close enough, I could smell the vanilla I'd gotten a whiff of earlier. I slowly, purposefully lowered my gaze to her mouth. Keeping it there for just a fraction too long before meeting her gaze again.

"Be seeing you, Baker."

Her lips parted—to throw more angry words my way, I was sure. But before a single sound escaped her, I spun on my heel, giving Justin's shoulder a squeeze before I hopped out. I retreated to a safe distance before turning around just in time to see Frankie refuse the wheelchair one of the nurses had rolled out.

She gave the thing one disgusted look before flicking her nose skyward and walking into the ER without any assistance. A chuckle rumbled its way through my chest. It was damn good to be back in Clearwater Bay.

No, scratch that. It was damn good to see Frankie again.

Now I just had to figure out how to get her in the same room as me so I could finally apologize to her.

Even if it meant risking my life.

3

FRANKIE

"What the actual hell, Frankie?"

Covering my yawn with the back of my hand, I opened the door wider. "Hello to you too, Maddie-Cakes."

"Oh no." She shook her head, her blonde ponytail furiously swishing back and forth. "Don't you *hello-to-you-too* me. You were supposed to get out of there! Instead, I have to find out from my fiancé that you were taken to the hospital because you were inside the bakery while it was on fire!"

The last couple of words came out of her mouth in a shriek and I had the good sense to feel a little bad. Okay, a lot bad. I was so worked up from seeing Gage that I headed straight home after I was given the *all-clear* at the ER.

By the time I realized I hadn't called anyone, it was almost 1 am and my phone was nowhere to be found. I figured it was still at the bakery.

Or what was left of it, I guessed.

"I'm sorry." I lifted my shoulders and dropped them again in a quick shrug. "Everything just happened so fast. One moment I was placing the muffins in the storeroom and the next I was on a gurney in the ambulance with someone trying to give me oxygen."

An image popped into my head right then. A very unwelcome image of a man with deep green eyes, an impossibly sexy grin, and an even sexier dimple. Ugh! That asshole had no right to the space he was taking up in my brain.

"Oh, Frankie! I'm just glad you're okay," Maddie breathed out a second before throwing her arms around me in a crushing hug. "I don't even—" she sniffled into my shoulder.

Maddie had been my soul sister from the moment she and I had stolen the boys' frisbee on the beach. She'd been four, and I was six and we'd been inseparable since. Not even the year we spent apart while she tried to pursue her dance career in New York could break the bond between us.

She was like a sister I never had. Hell, on most days I liked her more than I liked my actual brother.

So really, me not telling her I was okay was a massive dick move on my part. Especially since her fiancé, Adam had a very tragic past directly connected to a burning building.

Banding my arms tighter around her, I promised, "I'm really okay. They wouldn't have let me leave the ER if I wasn't." I held onto her upper arms as I gently pushed her away to look her in the eye. "Aren't I supposed to be the worrier in this relationship?"

"Well yeah," she wiped her nose with the side of her index finger. "That was before you turned into the one who does irresponsible things."

"Pffft," I scoffed as I turned around to head to the kitchen, knowing she'd be on my heels. "There was no way I could leave those delectable muffins and spilled frosting on the bench like that."

"Really? You couldn't leave because of *that*?"

I set to work on getting the coffee machine ready before I spun around to face her. "Hey, if you knew how freaking amazing those little morsels tasted, you'd understand." When her features didn't relax one bit, I added, "I thought I had more time, that's all." Giving her my back, I grabbed two mugs from the cabinet and pulled my emergency brownie stash from the cupboard.

When our coffees were prepared, I set the mugs along with the brownies on the island before slipping onto one of the stools. What I needed was for her to concentrate on something else.

Anything else.

Because as much as I loved my friend, I wasn't very fond of seeing her disappointed in me.

"So, uhhhhm." I took a small sip of my coffee. Mug still in hand, I eyed Maddie—who had finally taken a seat opposite me—over the rim. "Has Adam mentioned any newcomers to the station?"

Maddie pulled the container holding the brownies closer to her. After lifting the lid, she took a deep breath before pulling one out and taking a generous bite. "No, why?" she mumbled around a mouth full of cakey goodness.

She was in between chewing and swallowing when her hand flew up. "Oh wait, he did mention something about a new volunteer starting."

"Did he say who it was?"

She shook her head and chased the brownie down with some coffee while I set my mug on the counter. Finger mindlessly tracing the rim, I drew in a deep breath. Maddie was the only person, besides the asshole who was there, who knew what'd happened between me and Gage.

She'd been the one to pick up the pieces when he sped out of town like a bat out of hell while I was left feeling like a cheap whore. She was the one who kept me from going to his campus and giving him the third degree.

She was the one who finally convinced me he wasn't worth the precious gift I'd given him. She was also the one who understood why I had been doing my absolute best to avoid him since he got back almost a week ago.

"The firefighter who pulled me out was Gage," I blurted out.

"You're kidding?!" she cried, crumbs and coffee flying out of her mouth in every which way. "Gage? As in *Gage* Gage?"

"I only know one Gage," I answered solemnly.

"Well shit."

"You can say that again," I muttered pulling the brownies closer and stuffing almost the entire chocolatey square into my mouth. I chewed and chewed while Maddie's gaze roamed over my face in a way that made me feel like I had fire ants running around inside my panties.

"How was it seeing him after all this time?" she finally asked.

Unnerving. Mostly because he made every nerve ending in my body hum in approval. I wasn't about to admit that to the one person who hated the man almost as much I supposedly did. Washing down the last bite with a big gulp of coffee, I leaned forward and placed my folded arms on the counter.

"Honestly? It was weird." That wasn't a lie. "He's older, more distinguished, I guess. But somehow when I looked at him all I saw was that twenty-year-old not-yet-a-man-but-not-a-boy who broke my heart."

"Mhm." Maddie nodded and dragged the brownies back to her side. "You should break his nose for that."

I blinked and then promptly threw my head back and laughed.

"Wanna tell me what's so funny?"

"You," I told her as I wiped the happy tears from my eyes. "When exactly did you become so violent?"

Pinning me with a stare, she arched her eyebrow. "Dunno. I woke up a bit stabby since my best friend had me sick with worry all night."

"Maddie, I—"

"I know, I know," she gently interrupted. "I'll stop now. It's just, I'm a little more freaked out by fires after everything that happened with Adam."

I lifted my butt off the stool with the intention of going around the counter and hugging my friend, but I was in that awkward position between sitting and standing when loud bangs sounded against my front door.

Giving Maddie an apologetic look, I hurried to open the door before whoever was behind it broke it down. The whoever turned out to be my brother, Caden and he did not look happy to see me.

"What the hell?" he growled.

My lips stretched into a sweet smile—well, as sweet as I could muster—before I opened the door as wide as it would go. "That seems to be the question of the day."

"What?" my brother muttered as he stepped past me.

I shook my head at his broad back before closing the door and trailing behind him to the kitchen. As I knew he would, he was helping himself to a coffee and two brownies the instant he was inside.

"Well?" he asked impatiently as he wiped the crumbs from his beard and lowered his six-foot-four frame onto a stool next to Maddie. Giving her a sideways glance and a friendly smile, he greeted her.

"Hey, Maddie. How've you been?"

Her smile was sugary sweet. "Really good. How does it feel to be back home after being away for a decade?"

"Oh, you know—"

My gaze flicked between them. "Excuse me?" I huffed out. "Do you mind?" It was more than a little creepy how they both turned their heads to look at me at the same time. Or it would have been if Maddie didn't look about three seconds away from laughing her ass off while my idiot of a brother looked ready to commit murder.

Sounded like it to when he grunted out, "Huh?"

I crossed my arms in front of me and leaned my butt against the counter. "Did you forget your manners at home when you rushed over here to bang to your fists against your chest like an uncivilized gorilla?"

The veins in his forehead and neck looked like they were about to pop. "What the hell are you on about?"

"Why in shit's name were you trying to break down my door?"

"Don't give me that shit, Frankie." His frown deepened, and I was seriously worried about those veins. My kitchen would not look good covered in blood.

Ew, where did that thought come from?

"Why?" my brother bellowed, successfully interrupting my brain's weird thought-train. "Oh, I don't know. Maybe because I had to find out from my best friend that he had to pull you out of a burning building last night."

"Oh shit." This coming from Maddie who quickly took a way too big gulp of her coffee when I glared at her.

To Caden I said, "It was smoldering

"That's not what Gage sa—"

"Don't mention his name in my house!"

Caden threw his arms in the air and cursed. "For fuck's sake, Frankie. Now is not the time for this shit. I don't care about whatever thing is going on between you two. I only care about the fact that you could have been seriously hurt, and you didn't even let a single person know.

Not even Mom or Dad. They had to hear about it on the radio this morning when a local station reported about the fire and the buildings involved."

Apparently, I was a really crappy person. "Oh."

"Yeah, oh! And why the hell aren't you answering your phone?" He demanded, sounding every bit like the over-protective big brother. "We tried calling you the moment we found out."

Feeling a hell of a lot uncomfortable, I shifted from one foot to the other. Because I couldn't look him straight in the eye, my gaze bounced all over his face as I raked my fingers through my hair, wincing when I caught a tangle.

"I don't have my phone." My response sounded exactly like what it was. Weak. "I think it fell out of my pocket when I passed out on the storeroom floor. Everything happened so fast, Caden. I didn't think to call and let you guys know I was okay. Sorry."

His features softened. "We were worried sick. Me even more so when I saw the state of Sugar Booger this morning."

"Is it bad?" My heart didn't want to hear his answer because last night, even under the cover of smoke and darkness, it had looked bad. So very bad.

My brother scraped his palm over his neck. "It needs a lot of work. Your kitchen and about half of the front of the bakery won't be salvageable."

My knees felt weak. Uncrossing my arms, I shoved both hands into my hair. "How long will it take for you to fix it?" My brother's construction company—the one he co-owned with he-who-shall-not-be-named—was one of the best. They had built a great name and reputation that'd followed them from the big city all the way back to our little town.

In fact, that was the main reason they were back. The company had accepted an offer to build quite a few houses for some big shot businessman from Los Angeles who'd inherited a piece of land just outside of town.

"Mr. Dupree wants my full attention on the housing project. I probably won't even have time to wipe my ass for the next few months."

"Ew, I do not need that visual." Rubbing at my temples, a heavy blew over my lips. "How am—"

"Hang on, I didn't say Blue Ladder Construction wasn't going to work on it. You're my baby sister, it's a given that I am going to help rebuild your bakery…in one way or another." He sat up straight, a grin rivaling the one of the Cheshire cat spreading wide on his face. "I have the perfect man for the job."

The panic I'd felt moments ago morphed into something else entirely. From where I was standing, I glared at my brother willing him to feel the daggers I was shooting his way. While my brain was providing me with every cuss word I knew. Luckily, that wasn't what came out of my mouth.

"If it is who I think it is, you can forget about it."

4

GAGE

"Why can't I just stay home?"

I threw the truck in park and twisted my body to face my daughter. My daughter. I was still getting used to the sound of that. And not in a weird way either. I'd been fostering Maia for the better part of five years before I'd been able to legally adopt her a few months ago.

As far as broken childhoods went, Maia's had been up there. I'd gotten to know her when I started volunteering at the community center in Los Angeles after I quit firefighting. After what had happened, I'd felt lost and without purpose.

Then I saw this little girl sitting in the corner. Shoulders slumped like she was already carrying the weight of the world, she'd noodled in her sketchbook when two boys had walked up to her.

I could still remember the rush of protection that surged through me when those boys had spewed their ugly insults at her. I'd been three seconds away from stepping in when Maia looked up from her drawing and coolly told those boys off.

A sense of pride I'd had no right had washed over me then along with the need to know why this girl didn't have parents.

It was that need that drove me to talk with Mrs. Reiner, the social worker in charge of Maia's case. The first words she told me was that Maia might be in the system until she was eighteen because most families who were looking to adopt wanted babies or toddlers.

My heart had filled with so much sadness right then.

Mostly because my childhood was filled with great memories. I'd had the most wonderful parents who loved me and gave me everything I needed. And even though I'd lost them both when I'd been about Maia's age, there wasn't a say that hadn't felt cherished.

The thought of that young girl not having something even close to that had been devasting to me.

So much so that at the age of twenty-five and with no clue what the hell I was doing I'd decided I wanted to be the one to give her that. The journey that followed was anything but easy but one I'd take again in a heartbeat.

Because Maia was one damn amazing kid.

"Dad, you're being weird."

I blinked a few times until her face came into focus. Dark eyebrows pinched tightly over honey-colored eyes and her nose all scrunched up. She was looking at me like I'd grown a horn in the middle of my forehead.

It took me a moment to realize she'd asked me something before I took that sudden trip down memory lane.

"Weird is the new normal," I told her coolly. "And you can't stay home because you're not old enough to be by yourself."

She rolled her eyes in an overexaggerated way, a heavy sigh accompanying the action. "Geez, over-protective much? I turn thirteen in two months."

"Yes, Maia, I *am* over-protective." I reached across and squeezed her knee until she looked me in the eyes. "I would never forgive myself if anything happened to you. Besides, you staying here is more for Nan's benefit. She likes the company."

Maia snorted but the smile lifting her lips was genuine. "Nan has her telenovelas to keep her company and her friends from her crazy dance class."

"You know, you could probably join if you wanted to?"

"Ew Dad," she scoffed. "That class is for *old* people. And not old as you old but ancient like Nan."

I clutched at the left side of my chest. "Ouch. I am not old and there are all sorts of classes for kids your age," I said before sliding my arm along the bench to give her shoulder a meaningful squeeze. "It's going to take some time for both of us to get used to this new normal. I know the move was hard. Especially for you, Maia. I packed up our lives and moved us away from everything you knew. I just wanted a fresh start for us."

And I really wanted to give Frankie a long-overdue apology.

"Yeah," she breathed on an exhale.

As her gaze shifted from me to something beyond the windshield, I wondered yet again if I was doing the right thing. If this move had a negative impact on her, I would never be able to forgive myself.

Pushing the thought away for the time being, I gave her shoulder another squeeze and said, "Come on, let's get you inside. I have a meeting to get to." One that was going to be interesting as all hell if the other day was any indication to go by.

Maia and I were silent as we climbed out of the truck and made our way along the colorful cobblestone path. Looking around the yard as we went, I realized colorful was putting it mildly. It looked more like a rainbow had exploded on her front lawn.

Hip-high pink flamingos dotted the path along which we were walking. In a flower bed to the right were an array of *naughty* garden gnomes, doing things my daughter had no business seeing even though they were made of porcelain and no parts were visible.

To the left there were three monkeys sitting in a row. But instead of covering their eyes, ears, and mouths with both hands, they only had one on each respective part while flipping off the world with the other.

The two biggest trees in the yard had big-bulbed rainbow lights hanging from the branches with a sign stamped to one reading: *If you're selling something you can just turn around and fuck off.*

I'd seen it more than a hundred times in my lifetime and I still chuckled every time. Because that was Grandma Hes in a nutshell. Straight to the point, no-nonsense, and eccentric. But underneath all that, she had a heart of gold.

I was still shaking my head and laughing when the door swung open. The instant Nan stepped outside I quickly swallowed the gasp that wanted to break free. Maia wasn't as successful, though. Her eyes were almost as wide as her face, her hand covering her mouth. I could have sworn I'd heard her mutter "what the hell" under her breath. But that could've been me.

Completely unaware of the reaction she was evoking, Nan puffed out her chest and fluffed the ends of her bob hair.

Her pink and purple hair. "Well, what do you think? Mimi and I decided it was time for a change."

"It's…uh…" I dragged my fingers through my hair before scraping my palm over my chin. My gaze flicked to Maia. Her mouth was half-open, brows tightly pinched together. Yeah, she wasn't going to offer any help. "Interesting," I finally croaked out.

Unfazed by my reaction, Nan flicked her hair and clucked her tongue at me. "Oh hush you. Everyone is doing it. It's the new fashion. But I don't expect you to understand because you, Gage Calloway wouldn't know fashion even if it bit you in the ass."

"Nan!"

Her eyes snapped to Maia, her features immediately softening. "Bum. I mean, bum," she amended with a wink.

Shaking her head, Maia snort-laughed before hugging first me then Nan before she disappeared into the house. I waited until she was out of sight before I turned my attention to my grandma again.

"I told you no cussing in front of Maia."

Nan motioned for me to bend down so she could tap a shaky hand against my cheek. "Have you had some action recently? I hear it's a very successful way to remove the stick from your *bum*." She leaned in closer like she was about to divulge a juicy secret. "And word on the street is Frankie still isn't seeing anyone."

"Nan!" Straightening, I took a step back and scowled.

My grandma just smiled sweetly and shrugged. "Don't Nan me. She's a lovely girl and the pair of you would look so adorable together." The sigh escaping her lips sounded dreamy. "And the babies! They would be absolutely perfect."

Since my teenage years, Nan had been on me about Frankie. Always telling me what a lovely girl she was or making some remark about how I should make my move before someone else did. Being the dipshit I was, I never did make that move. Frankie did.

Right before I screwed everything up.

Stopping that thought in its tracks, I bent down to kiss Nan's cheek. "I hate to cut your trip to dreamland short but I gotta go. Love you, Nan."

I was out of the yard and in my truck before she had time to utter another word. Because I didn't need my Nan to tell me how great Frankie and I could be together. I already knew.

It might've been just for one night, but everything about it was burned into my soul. Every breath, every sound, the way she moved. I remembered it all. As stupid as it might sound, that one night changed my life.

Shaking my head at myself, I turned the key until the engine rumbled to life. With one last look at Nan's house to make sure she went inside, I pulled away from the curb and headed toward Main street.

The closer I got the more pungent the stench of smoke and rubble became until I turned right onto Main Street and the damage of the night before became visible. It sure as shit looked a lot more devastating in the light of day.

The more buildings—or at least what was left of them—I passed the harder my heart slammed against my ribs. If the rest of the street looked like this, I could only imagine what Frankie's bakery looked like.

Tearing my gaze away from the crowds of people gathered around the buildings, I tightened my hold on the steering wheel. It was so easy to forget how destructive something so mesmerizing could be.

One breath was all it took for the flames to reach higher, burn hotter and destroy anything in its path. It didn't care who you were or how hard you'd worked. All it wanted to do was run wild. Be free.

It was one of the main reasons why I had such a deep-rooted respect for the flames. It was also the reason why I was scared shitless of it too. I'd been on both sides. Seen the beauty, survived the destruction.

Hell. I'd even walked away from it for a long time. But the call of the fire was one siren song I could no longer ignore.

With a sharp shake of my head, I forced my thoughts back to the present just in time to see Frankie's bakery come into view. She was already there; arms hugged tight around her waist as she listened to whatever Caden was saying.

She didn't look upset, and I wondered if she even knew I was overseeing this project since her brother would be busy with the Engiss Enterprises deal. The deal that had landed us back in Clearwater Bay.

Although, I probably would have made this move even if Arthur Engiss hadn't given the contract to Blue Ladder Construction. Coming back here and making my wrongs right moved to the top of my list the moment Maia and I officially became a family.

As if she could feel my eyes on her, Frankie's head slowly turned my way. I swear, the instant our eyes locked it was me and her and nothing else. The glass, the distance, none of it was there.

It was just her blue gaze burning into mine.

And burn it did. One look and I felt hot all over. The heat in my veins causing my skin to feel tight. Almost too tight. My heart picked up speed, slamming against my ribs like a caged animal trying to make its escape.

It'd been years. Ten years for shit's sake. And still, she was the only woman who could evoke such a visceral reaction in me.

Not that she knew. And judging by the way her beautiful mouth pressed into tight thin line, the feeling most definitely wasn't mutual. I didn't care too much. She had no idea how sinfully sexy she was when she was riled up and ready for a fight.

A fight I was all too willing to give her because breaking down her defenses and earning her trust again was going to be fan-fucking-tastic.

After running my fingers through my hair, I schooled my features and climbed out of my truck. No sooner had my feet hit the ground before Frankie twisted around and came stomping my way.

Biting back my grin, I dug my heels in and waited.

"Get in your stupid truck and go back into the hole you crawled out of," she growled the moment she was in front of me.

One corner of my mouth slowly tipped up. "So feisty. Did someone forget to drink their happy juice this morning?"

"Dammit, Gage! Go away."

I folded my arms in front of my chest and got a kick out of her eyes widening when they followed the movement. "Who's going to restore your pretty little bakery if I leave, Baker?"

"I don't care." She mirrored my stance, pushing her breasts out like an offering ready to be devoured. "As long as it's not you!"

I took a step forward, vanilla immediately filling my senses. I wanted to lean down and flick my tongue over her skin just to find out if she tasted of it too. Shit, if I kept thinking things like this I was going to find myself in a rather…hard situation.

Reigning in my thoughts for a moment, I let my gaze roam over her face. “Ah, but you know I’m the best.”

Frankie’s eyes dropped to my mouth for a long hot second before she tilted her chin up in a defiant manner. “I’ve seen better.”

Oh, have you, now? Why don’t I just throw you over the hood of my truck and show you how—

“I don’t know what the hell is going on here,” Caden successfully interrupted my thoughts. “but whatever it is, can you two cut it out so we can discuss what needs doing?” The look he gave me right then warned me we were going to have a talk later.

One I probably wasn’t going to like.

5

FRANKIE

Stupid freaking Gage!

Ugh, if ever there was a man who could ruffle my feathers it was him. I mean really, who the hell did he think he was? Waltzing in here looking like *that*? I wanted to smack the stupid sexy grin off his face right after I handed him a shirt two sizes too big so I wouldn't have to look at his obnoxiously chiseled chest.

Asshole.

"What do you think?"

My brother's voice sliced through the thick fog covering my brain. I blinked to clear the rest of it away only to find two pairs of eyes expectantly staring at me. Now if only I could recall what we were talking about.

Tapping my chin with my finger, I tilted my head sideways and pretended to think it over. What I really needed was for one of these two idiots to come to my rescue because I had no desire to explain to either of them I'd been lost in freaking la-la land while they were talking about the rebuild.

"It makes the most sense," Gage finally said. "You never know when something like this can happen again, so having the fireproof walls is a must."

Why did his voice have to sound so gritty and sinful while he was talking about walls? Walls weren't freaking sexy. *No, but Gage sure is*, a little voice in the back of my mind sing-songed.

That bitch needed to shut the hell up because we weren't going there today…or tomorrow.

Or at all.

Glaring at him, I bit out, "Why are you still here?"

Being the asshole he was, he shoved his hands in his pockets and grinned while his eyes slowly traveled up and down the length of me. He was just looking at me but somehow managed to set my body on fire.

I wasn't sure if I wanted to slap him or sit on him.

"We've been over this, Frankie," my brother said, managing to sound both exasperated and amused at the same time. "Gage is staying. Now, can we get back to it because I have a meeting with Mr. Engiss in a couple of hours."

What was it about big brothers that made you want to turn into a teenage version of yourself just so you could stick out at him? Or maybe that was just me.

Huffing out a "Fine," I flicked my gaze to the spot where the walls needed to go.

"Fireproof walls it is. Anything else you absolutely insist I must have?" I turned my attention back to the guys just in time to see Gage drag his hand over the back of his neck. The action not only pulled me out of my thoughts but also made his bicep pop deliciously. How wonderful would it have been to just curl my fingers around the thick muscle and hang on for days and days.

Oh, for the love of—

"I'm sure I can talk Bob from Gyproc into giving us a special price," Caden mused as his fingers flew over his phone. Once he was done typing, he slipped the device back into his pocket.

"And if anything else comes up Gage will be more than happy to go over it with you."

I narrowed my eyes in Gage's direction. "Of course he will." Completely ignoring the snark in my tone, his grin stretched wider and his stupid dimples appeared.

"So that's settled then." Caden clapped his hands together. "We'll have the cleanup crew in here tomorrow morning first thing." Turning in a slow circle, he took one last look at the place before wrapping me up in an unexpected hug. "I give you my word, Sugar Booger's doors will be open in no time."

Emotion clogged up my throat and caused my eyes to sting. Not just at the genuineness in Caden's tone but also at the reality of the situation slamming into me. This place wasn't just a business. I'd put my heart and my soul into this. Everything that left that kitchen held a piece of me. An important piece.

And now it was reduced to rubble.

I had complete faith that my brother and even Gage would work their hands to the bone to restore Sugar Booger to its former glory. I just needed to figure out what to do with myself until then. Cause I was starting to feel a hell of a lot lost.

Swallowing down the somber thoughts, I pushed onto my toes and kissed Caden's cheek. "Thank you." Pulling back, I gave him a smile. "Don't tell anyone but you're my favorite brother."

The corners of his mouth tipped up even as he rolled his eyes. "I'm your *only* brother."

"Eh, you say potato, I say po-tah-to. Now away with you."

With a sharp shake of his head, Caden snort-laughed and headed out, mumbling something about little sisters as he went.

I couldn't help but smile until I felt Gage move behind me. How on earth did I forget he was there?

"I can't wait to start working you."

Pulling my brows together, I spun around. He was standing so close I almost slammed into him. "What did you say?"

That annoying half-smirk was back. "I can't wait to start working on this for you. I know how important this place is."

"How could you possibly know?" *You weren't here for the last ten years, remember? You took me for a damn fool right before you split town faster than overwhipped cream.*

There was barely any space between us, still, he took a step forward. The blunt edges of his work boots pressing against the tips of my sandal-covered toes. Tilting his head, Gage's eyes roamed over my face. Studying me in a way that made me want to fidget.

When he finally opened his mouth to speak, I got the impression the words that tumbled out weren't the ones he wanted to say. "See you tomorrow." His gaze dropped to my lips for a second too long before he leaned in close. Close enough that his warm breath fanned my cheek with every whispered word. "Don't miss me too much."

"Ugh." My hands shot out to shove the obnoxious dick, but he jumped out of the way before I made contact. Squaring my shoulders, I folded my arms in front of me. "Oh, believe me, I won't. Out of sight, out of mind. That's how it goes, isn't it?"

Something happened to his face then. A mixture of pain and guilt broke to the surface before he had time to school his features. It was fast and I would have missed it if I hadn't been looking at him so intently.

"Fra—"

"I'd love to stand here and make niceties with you…" I interrupted him. "Well, actually no, I wouldn't. Goodbye Gage." My heart slammed against my ribs as I rushed away from the bakery like some speed demon. Unfortunately, in my effort to get away from Gage as far and fast as possible, I almost plowed over poor Susan from the coffee shop down the street. "I'm so sorry," I stammered, gripping her upper arms to keep her from toppling over.

"No worries. I was actually looking for you."

"Oh?" Releasing her, I took a step back as she smoothed her clothes back into place.

Susan stared at a spot over my shoulder, her ginger brows slowly creeping together. I was about to turn around to see what held her attention when she finally looked at me and spoke. "I'm so sorry about Sugar Booger. You must be devastated."

No. I'm throwing a freaking party in my head. Biting my cheek, I kept the sarcasm from spilling over my lips. It really wasn't her fault I was in a piss poor mood. Nope, that had Gage written all over it.

Giving her as sweet a smile as I could muster, I said, "It's not ideal but at least I'm finally getting to those renovations I've been putting off."

By the way Susan threw her head back and howled you'd have thought I'd told the world's funniest joke. I wasn't sure how I felt about that. Maybe keeping my sarcasm inside hadn't been the best decision.

"That's so you, Francesca," she finally managed once her breathing evened out. "Always looking on the bright side of everything. We could all use a dose of that in our lives."

Well, shit. Now I felt bad. And a little mad too. Because somehow in the space of a few hours I'd turned into this PMS monster without actually having PMS. Maybe I was close, though?

"I hate to bring it up at a time like this," Susan went on, blissfully unaware of the crazy talk going on inside my brain. "But a few of our customers were already asking about your delicious treats. Do you know when you'll have a delivery for us again?"

Just hearing those words brought on a bout of nausea. Businesses like Morning Kick made up a big part of my monthly income. There was no way I could sit still and do nothing while the bakery was being rebuilt. Firstly, I was a firm believer in idle hands being the devil's playground. I might end up texting someone I definitely didn't need to be texting.

And secondly—most importantly—I would lose clients. People like Susan would have to look elsewhere to stock their shelves. Yeah, maybe some of them would come back once Sugar Booger was open again, but that really wasn't a risk I was willing to take.

Then it hit me.

"I can always bake from home while Sugar Booger is closed. My permits are still valid. And since there are only certain things I am permitted to bake from my home kitchen, I won't be able to offer you your normal order but definitely enough to keep the customers from rioting. Would that be okay?"

Susan lit up like a 100-megawatt light bulb. "Whatever you can manage would be fantastic. You know everyone in this town just adores your treats."

"Great." A little fire flickered to life inside me. "I'll give Misty a call and we'll get started as soon as possible. With any luck, I might have something for you by tomorrow afternoon."

After we said our goodbyes, I rushed to my car with renewed energy.

Maybe just maybe this was the silver lining to my little dark cloud.

6

FRANKIE

"Wow, I can't believe we actually made all of these."

I leaned back against the sink and looked at the treats covering my kitchen counters. Misty and I had been elbow deep in flour, butter, and sugar since 5 am. We were completely exhausted.

Exhausted but happy.

During the span of 6 hours we'd managed to get out four dozen cupcakes, seven trays of brownies, and two dozen bagels—I'd prepared the dough and formed them the previous night.

Even though this wasn't close to what we made on a normal day at Sugar Booger, it was something. And spending time with my hands stuck in dough or covered with creamy frosting made me feel not so blah.

Plus it took my mind off everything else going on.

Like the bakery and how long it would be before it was up and running again. Or Gage and his stupid muscles and obnoxious smile that made my tummy flip. Yeah, I definitely needed a distraction and baking was the best kind there was.

"We did good." I elbowed Misty and her grin grew wide. "You should go home and get some rest. I'll pack these up and take them down to Morning Kick."

Her shoulders slumped with relief but still, she asked, "Are you sure? I can totally take these to Susan for you." Misty had one of those voices that kind of needed to grow on you. It was shrill and high-pitched and apparently, it reached new heights when she was tired.

"Positive. You can do the delivery tomorrow while I kick back with a fruity drink in my hand and some Jo-bros in my ears."

Shaking her head, she pushed off the counter and trudged toward the entryway. "You and your Jonas Brothers. There are way bands to listen to."

I clutched my chest in mock-horror. "How dare you? No other band can come close to my precious Jo-bros. They're adorable with voices of angels and I just want to pinch their cheeks."

Her head was still shaking as she exited the kitchen with a muttered, "You're so weird."

I swear, she could thank her lucky stars that she was such an amazing employee. I had disowned people for far less because really, I didn't need that kind of negativity in my life. That's exactly why I pulled out my phone and popped my buds into my ears before hitting play on my favorite playlist.

A little over an hour later, with endorphins coursing through my veins and treats stacked in my arms I walked into Morning Kick. I'd barely cleared the door when Susan came rushing toward me.

"There you are." Before I could hand them to her, she snatched the containers from me and hurried back to the counter where she immediately started filling the display cases.

Display cases that emptied faster than she could restock them.

Warmth spread through my being and I was reminded of one of the reasons why I loved to bake. I wasn't artistic in the way Maddie was. She could bring people to tears or laughter with her dancing. She touched them in ways they never knew they could be touched.

But somehow I could bring a smile to someone's lips by giving them a sweet treat. The way their eyes would widen at that first bite always felt like an adrenaline shot to the heart.

This was what I lived for.

I was still smiling like a freaking idiot when I felt eyes on me. Turning my head slightly, my gaze immediately collided with Gage's from across the vast space. I didn't want to see him. Didn't want him to taint this little piece of heaven I found myself in.

Spinning on my heels, I got out of there as fast as I could. It still wasn't fast enough.

"Frankie, wait!"

Seriously?! I hadn't seen this man once in ten years and now all of a sudden he was freaking everywhere. And why oh why for the love of all things holy did he have to say my name like that? Gritting my teeth, I spun around and parked my hands on my hips. "What? What do you want, Gage? Hmm?"

I wasn't expecting it, so when one corner of his mouth quirked, I couldn't really blame my heart for doing that pitter-patter thing again. Because the man looked all kinds of delicious with those full lips stretched into a half-smirk.

"You look good. How have you been?" His voice, smooth yet somehow gritty, glided over my body, burning up my veins as it went.

I spared him an incredulous look for all of two seconds before I turned around again. Only this time he didn't call after me. Oh no, the asshole curled his fingers around my arm and almost tugged me flush against his chest.

His incredibly broad and beautifully sculpted chest.

Needing space from this man and all the havoc he was causing to my insides, I yanked my arm out of his grasp and stepped back. "What the hell do you think you're doing?"

"I want to apologize for the way I left."

Those green eyes pierced through my soul, the intensity of it reminding me of the hurt and humiliation he'd caused me. Not that I needed reminding, I carried that with me every damn day.

Even while I'd been in my first and only serious relationship, it had been there. *He'd* been there. The one man I could never get out of my system.

Well, no more.

Lifting my chin, I glared at him. "You've apologized now leave me alone."

"Do you think we could talk sometime?" he went on as if I hadn't just told him to go to hell. "Maybe I can take you out to dinner?"

"Maybe instead of dinner you should use the time and see an ear doctor because yours have clearly stopped working."

My words must've amused him because his grin was back. "So serious. All that tension can't be good for you."

"Excuse me?"

The bastard licked his lips before taking a step closer to me. As much as I didn't want him in my space, there was no way in hell I was going to give him the satisfaction of shrinking back.

I stood taller instead and tilted my head to meet his stare.

"Your mouth says one thing," he murmured, "but your eyes…they tell an entirely different story."

The air around us sizzled, trapping my breath inside my lungs. My lips parted to talk, to suck in air…I didn't know. But the moment my mouth opened; Gage's eyes zeroed in on the action.

His dark green irises focused on me with so much intensity, it made my skin feel alive. Like a million little ants were crawling all over me with no sense of direction. I wanted to scratch and rub at it.

Or maybe he could do it for me?

This was beyond freaking ridiculous. I wanted to tap my fingers against my chest to remind the traitor behind my ribcage of the first time it had hurt. Because this man with his panty-melting grin and soul-searching eyes had been the cause of that pain.

He was the reason why I didn't trust men. To be fair, Rick the dick was the main reason why my faith in the opposite sex was non-existent. But Gage wasn't innocent either. Not by a long freaking shot.

"Frankie?"

At the sound of the familiar voice I sighed with relief while Gage's brows pulled together. In less than a second, his smile dissolved, and he aimed his scowl at something over my shoulder.

I took a quick breath before pivoting and almost choked on a laugh. Because what were the chances of me running into Gage and then Brian, the guy I stood up the other night. Although I did feel that couldn't be held against me since I was passed out inside the storeroom of a burning building.

"I thought that was you," Brian said, his voice cheerful.

Reaching behind me, I pulled my braid over my shoulder. Toying with the ends, I pasted a smile on my lips. "Yeah…I'm sorry about the other night. The bake—"

"I know." His features softened. "I tried calling you today and when your phone kept sending me to voicemail, I swung by your bakery."

A snort from behind me reminded me that Gage was still there. Not that I really needed to be reminded. I could feel his presence behind me like a big looming shadow. My brain felt jittery, my nerve endings on high alert. *Why is he affecting me like this? And more importantly, why is he still here?*

Turning my head sideways, I attempted to glare at him. It didn't really work considering the angle, so I added a little bite to my tone. "Don't you have somewhere you need to be?"

"Nah, I'm good." He took another step closer, the warmth of his body seeping into my pores almost immediately. I had to fight the sudden urge to close my eyes and lean back against his hard chest.

"Why don't you introduce me to your friend, Baker?" The gritty timbre of his voice rolled over my skin and I hated him for making me feel this way.

"Go away, Gage."

"Brian. Nice to meet you."

Brian and I spoke at the same time. Even though what I did probably sounded a lot more like hissing instead of talking.

Rather than stepping out behind me, Gage reached around me to shake Brian's hand. His arm brushed mine and I swear I felt electricity pulse in my veins. How on earth could such a small touch evoke such big feelings?

"Gage," the man behind me grumbled. He snatched back his hand but made no move to step back. Great. Just freaking great.

Meanwhile, Brain's gaze flicked from me to Gage before settling on me again. "So…uh…I was hoping we could reschedule since our last dinner date didn't pan out so great."

Ignoring another snort behind me, I smiled at Brian. He was a good-looking guy. Tall, I would've guessed about four inches shorter than Gage's six-foot-four. Sandy hair, bright blue eyes, and a smile that could light up a room.

A few days ago the idea of going out with this man and possibly ending up in his bed sounded so enticing. Then the asshat glowering behind me showed up and my entire world flipped. How the hell was that even possible?

I had to get back some sense of normal. I just had to.

"Yeah, that sounds great." This time there was no snort from Gage but rather a low growl. "If you could write your number down for me, I'll give you a call as soon as I get my phone situation sorted."

Still smiling, he reached into his pocket and pulled out a business card. His gaze flicked to Gage for a quick second before he handed me the card. "I look forward to finally having that dinner with you, Frankie."

"Yeah, me too." Why did the words taste like acid coming out? Lowering my eyes, I chose to aim my frown at the card in my hand. As I carefully studied the bold letters printed in black, a feeling of dread slithered down my spine and settled in the pit of my stomach.

Why the hell was I feeling like this?

"I gotta go," Brian said. "Nice meeting you, Gage."

I looked up in time to see Brian smile and wave before ambling down the sidewalk and disappearing around the corner. Nibbling on my lip, I willed the awful feeling that'd taken ahold of me to just go the hell away.

The wish fairies must've been having a freaking off day because the dread coating my insides was replaced with warmth when Gage leaned over my shoulder and his woodsy scent wrapped around me like a hug. A yummy yet very unwelcome hug. "Brian Rogers, IT analyst." The words came out in a low sexy grumble. "You're not really going out with this guy, are you?"

This time when I turned around, it was slow and steady. Gage was still invading my space so when I tilted my chin upward, our faces were mere inches apart. Jaw ticking, nostrils flaring, his eyes searched mine.

There was a time when all I wanted to do was get lost in the depths of those green irises. When I needed him to look at me like he was right now. Then he used my body and broke my heart.

I had to remember that.

Drawing strength from every ounce of hatred I felt for this man, I let the words roll off my tongue. "Whether I have dinner with Brian or let him screw me senseless is none of your damn business." With that I spun around and walked off, feeling extremely proud of myself for not looking back even once.

7

GAGE

As desperately as every cell in my being called out to me to follow Frankie as she stomped down the sidewalk, I knew I couldn't. She needed a little more time and space to come to terms with my presence.

I could respect that. Hell, I could even give her that—to a certain extent of course, because staying away from her would be impossible.

What I couldn't do was like it.

Grinding my teeth together, I stood rooted to the spot until Frankie slipped into her car and disappeared into the afternoon's busy traffic. Well, as busy as small-town traffic could get.

When she was nothing more than a speck in the sun; I headed to my truck. Slamming the door with a little more force than was needed. Once I was seated behind the steering wheel, I turned the key in the ignition a bit harder than was necessary too. And when the engine finally roared to life, I shoved my truck into gear with so much vehemence, the gearbox screeched in response.

It probably wasn't the smartest idea to take out my irritation on my only means of transport, but it was either that or smash in Brian the dickwad's face. As damn fantastic as it would have been to do the latter, I really couldn't afford to.

Not with the adoption still so fresh.

And definitely not with me trying to get a permanent gig at the fire station.

Sucking in a ragged breath, I forced my mind to go anywhere else but seeing as it was where my stubbornness stemmed from, it stayed firmly stuck on Frankie and the dickwad.

What the hell did she even see in him?

All suited and tied with his polished shoes and perfectly styled hair, he was everything she wasn't…in the worst possible way. The Frankie I knew had a spirit so free, no man would've ever been able to tame it. She'd been fun and spontaneous with a personality so big; it could never fit into one space.

This giant force of nature that you just wanted to be a part of.

That was Frankie.

"Shit," I groaned as I rolled to a stop in the Blue Ladder Construction parking lot just outside of town. Not staying and telling her how I really felt was my biggest regret. But in that same breath I knew if I'd stayed, my life would've turned out so different.

I might have had Frankie, but I wouldn't have had my daughter. And Maia was without a doubt the best thing that'd happened to me.

Heaving out a sigh, I unfolded myself from the truck. Closing the door in a much gentler way before I dragged my ass inside.

"Finally! I'm starved," Caden said as I walked through the door. When I just looked at him, his features turned worried. Eyes frantically scanning me over, he asked, "Dude, where's the food?"

With a muttered curse, I dragged my hands over my face and shoved my fingers through my hair. The moment I had seen Frankie flee the coffee shop, my only thought had been to catch up with her.

Clearly, I'd forgotten why I'd been there in the first place.

"Shit man," I blew out a breath. "I ran into Frankie and kinda got distracted."

Caden leaned back in his seat and studied me through narrowed eyes. "Hmm, I see."

"What's that look for?" Ignoring the beautiful view of the beach and ocean beyond the wall of windows behind my friend, I lowered myself onto the black wingback in front of his desk. Folding my arms in front of me, I asked, "Wanna tell me what's going on with your face right now?"

He studied me for a long, silent moment before he leaned forward and rested his folded arms on his desk. "You and I have been friends for the better part of XX years, right?" When I just grunted in agreement he went on, "Not once did I tell you to stay away from my sister. I've always felt Frankie could date whoever she wanted; I was just on standby to beat up the asshole who hurt her."

"Where exactly are you going with this, Caden?"

His nostrils flared with the slow breath he released. "I know something happened between the two of you all those years ago." I must not have hidden my shock very well, because he let out a snort. "I'm pretty sure everyone knows, man. You were in a piss poor mood almost every day for a few years. And so was my sister. Plus, you stopped coming home with me for long weekends and holidays."

Caden lifted his shoulders in a shrug. "It wasn't that hard to put two and two together."

If he only knew what exactly had happened, he wouldn't have been so damn calm about it. I'm positive if a boy ever did to Maia what I did to Frankie, I'd hunt him down, cut out his balls before shoving it down his throat.

Just the thought that this was the kind of punishment I deserved sent shockwaves to my groin.

"It took a while," Caden continued. "but Frankie eventually met someone. I didn't care too much for Rick for no other reason than he was the preppy kind who wouldn't be caught dead throwing back beers at the local watering hole. But he made my sister happy, and that was all that mattered to me."

I bit down on my back teeth to the point of pain. I knew about Rick the dick. Somewhere along the line, I'd needed to hear Frankie's voice as much as I needed to take my next breath.

It was that need that drove me to pick up the phone and call her. Only she didn't answer, *he* did. And when I not-so-politely asked him who he was, I got a sobering slap in the face when he told me.

That thumping thing inside my chest had taken a hell of a beating that day. Because there she was going on with her life while I'd been so stuck and unable to move past her. Not that it'd been her fault.

Of course, I couldn't tell Caden any of this so I kept my ass firmly planted on the chair and listened to what he had to say.

"They were together for five years. My mother was already planning the wedding and naming the babies when everything went to shit. Frankie wasn't feeling well and had decided to close the bakery early. Unfortunately, her day got a whole lot worse when she got home and found Rick buried balls deep inside his father's secretary."

"Fuck"

I was vaguely aware of Caden talking but I couldn't hear anything past the blood-red anger coursing through my veins. My brain was already calculating the different ways in which I could get more information on this shithead while my fingers itched to rearrange his face.

The damn excuse of a man didn't deserve to breathe.

It was only when I heard Caden's chuckle that I realized I'd said that last part out loud. "I felt the same way when Frankie told us what happened. I was ready to give the cheating asshole an ass whooping he'd never forget."

My brows pulled together. "You didn't?"

"Nah. Only because she threatened to never share her baked treats with me again. Rick the dick wasn't worth never having one of Frankie's cupcakes again."

It was my turn to chuckle because I completely understood Caden's view on the matter. If there was one thing Frankie excelled at—besides driving me insane with lust—it was baking.

I could still see a sixteen-year-old Frankie, covered in flour, traipsing around her mom's kitchen, trying out different recipes and forcing her brother and me to taste them. Even back then I knew she was something special. Knew that girl was going to ruin my heart for anyone else.

But being as young and stupid as I was, I didn't understand the ramification of such feelings. And I sure as shit didn't know what to do with them.

If only I had, maybe just maybe—

The sound of Caden's chair squeaking pulled me out of my thoughts in time to see him pushing to his feet. He rounded the desk and seated his ass against the edge in front of me. “I didn’t tell you any of this because I wanted to go all big brother on your ass and warn you to stay away from my sister. That’s not how I do things. I want you to know if you plan on pursuing Frankie, I won’t stand in your way. But if you hurt her again, the fact that I care for you like a brother won’t mean shit.”

“I appreciate you saying that.” Clearing my throat, I straightened out of the chair. “Because your sister is the reason why I came back to Clearwater Bay.”

8

FRANKIE

On any normal day dropping by my parents' place would have excited me. Today though, nerves ate at me with every step I took toward their front door. Because I felt terrible over all the worry I'd caused them.

After sucking in a quick breath, I dragged my palms over my denim-clad thighs before poking the little bell button next to the door. The melody from inside the house hadn't even had a chance to die down before the door flew open and my mom launched herself at me.

Good thing she was tiny otherwise we would've ended up on a heap on the floor. "We were so worried when we heard the news and couldn't reach you," she said against my hair.

"I know. I'm sorry."

My mom pulled back just as my dad appeared in the doorway behind her. "Thank heavens you're all right." I saw the relief on his face as much as I heard it in his voice. And for whatever reason, it pushed me over the edge.

My throat felt thick and scratchy as tears stung the back of my eyes. Blinking furiously, I willed the emotion to go the hell away. But much like everything else today, nothing went the way I wanted.

In the space of a breath, thick hot tears spilled over my lids and ran down my cheeks. My chest ached with a pain I hadn't felt in a very long time and a feeling of hopelessness settled in the pit of my stomach.

Just when I thought I couldn't possibly get any more emotional both my mom and dad wrapped their arms around me. It was one of those hugs that slowly filled your body with warmth. One that comforted and reassured without words.

One I had no idea I needed.

"Come on," my dad murmured after who knew how long. "Let's get you inside. What you need now is a stiff drink and your mama's cooking." Then he wiped the tears from my face and kissed me on the forehead. "Everything is going to be just fine."

Because I was still feeling all kinds of emotional, I didn't trust myself to speak. Instead, I gave my parents a quick nod and a too-wide smile that probably made me look like a deranged serial killer before gingerly trudging behind them into the house.

Once we reached the kitchen, I had to close my eyes and inhale deeply. The smell of garlic and bacon hung in the air, instantly filling me with a homey feeling. "Mmm, you made Carbonara."

After taking another big whiff of Mom's cooking, I opened my eyes and slipped onto one of the stools at the kitchen island. My smile couldn't be helped as I watched my mom and dad seamlessly work around each other in the kitchen.

Mom was finishing up the dish by slowly stirring in the yolks while my dad gathered the ingredients for his favorite drink. Every time he needed to push past my mom for something, he'd lay a hand on the small of her back or kiss her on top of the head.

In return my mom would beam at him like he was her entire world.

I would never admit it out loud but even though my heart had been battered and bruised and my trust in men was non-existent, I still wanted what my parents had. Wanted a man to look at me the way my dad looked at my mom. I wanted to know what it would feel like to love and trust so completely that it bubbled out of your pores for the entire world to see.

"If you're not careful, steam is going to come out of your ears."

I blinked back to reality only to find my dad standing opposite me with glasses and the ingredients he'd gathered already set out on the surface of the island. "Tell me again about how you and Mom met."

"Don't you know it by heart already?"

I leaned forward. Balancing my elbow on the island top, I rested my chin in my palm. "Tell me anyway."

With a shake of his gray head, he pulled the bourbon closer. His elderly hands had a slight tremble to them as he unscrewed the cap and poured about two fingers' worth of amber liquid into the glasses.

"Well," he started when he traded the bourbon bottle for the ginger beer. "I was working as a barman on this fancy cruise ship. There was a mix-up of some sort that day and I ended up manning the poolside bar instead of the one in the dining area."

My eyes flicked to his hands as he filled the glasses halfway with the ginger beer. When that was done, he added a few shakes of bitters to the drinks then halved a lemon while thinly slicing the other one.

"I was about to demand they move me to where I was supposed to be," he went on. "because I was finally going to ask out this girl I'd been making eyes at for almost three days. Then it happened. The prettiest girl I'd ever laid eyes on walked up to the bar looking like an angel."

He touched his palm to his chest. "My heart started beating so fast, I thought I was dying. Then she smiled and my entire world flipped upside down. So much so that I hadn't even noticed the man standing beside her."

"Oh yeah, mom was set to marry that banker guy…what was his name again?" I snapped my fingers while random names popped out of my mouth. "Jerry. Jerome. Justin."

"Martin," my mom provided dryly. "Your granddaddy moved heaven and earth to arrange that engagement but one look at your father and I just knew I was going to disappoint mine terribly."

I'd seen it a million times but the way my dad lit up at my mom's words made me feel all warm and fuzzy inside. "And all because Dad made you his famous horsefeather."

"I'd like to think my charm had something to do with it too," my dad chimed in. After squeezing a generous amount of lemon juice into each glass, he stirred the concoction and topped it with a few slices of lemon before sliding one over to me.

I took a big gulp and grinned. "It was definitely the drink, Dad."

My dad pretended to be taken aback for all of two seconds before he threw his head back and laughed. The sound was infectious, my mom and I had no other choice than to join in.

It was also the time I realized how wrong my dad was. I didn't need a stiff drink, I just needed this. Being around them was all the comfort my soul craved. I set my drink down and slipped off the stool. Once I'd made my way around the island, I threw my arms around my dad and hugged him tightly.

We stood like that for a few seconds before I pulled back and joined my mom at the stove. I hooked my arm through hers and rested my head on her shoulder. Using my free hand, I attempted to steal pasta from the pot.

"When's Caden coming, I'm starving."

Mom clicked her tongue and shoved my hand away so she cover the pot. "He should be here any minute now."

The words had barely left her mouth when the doorbell chimed. Smiling sweetly, she patted my cheek before hurrying out of the kitchen. While she opened the door for my brother my dad and I got the plates and cutlery ready.

"Soooo." The amused tone of my dad's voice had me looking from the open drawer I'd been rummaging in. Studying me over the rim of his glass, his blue eyes sparkled with mirth.

I quirked a brow. "So?"

"Your brother tells me Gage will be overseeing the construction at the bakery."

Ugh! Fantastic. "Uh, yeah, he is."

"And you're okay with it?"

Suddenly feeling uncomfortable, I focused on pulling forks and knives out of the drawer. "Of course. Why wouldn't I be?"

I hadn't expected my dad to move so silent or fast, so when he appeared next to me and placed his hand on my shoulder I got such a big fright I jolted and dropped the hand full of cutlery back into the drawer.

"Geez, Dad."

Not caring that he just scared the crap out of me, he squeezed my shoulder and said, "The last time anyone mentioned his name in front of you, you all but ran out of the room." He leaned closer. "And that was a couple of weeks ago."

I'd never been very good at hiding things from my dad. Way back when Gage had left town my dad had been one of the first ones to notice that something was wrong. He'd taken me out for a milkshake and asked what had happened.

Naturally, I'd refused to talk about it and being the awesome person that he was, he hadn't pushed. All he'd said was, "Everything gets better with time. Even broken hearts." And that had been that.

Sighing, I lifted my gaze to meet his. "It'll be fine."

His eyes bore into mine. He did not look convinced at all. "There's a fine line between love and hate. So fine that it's easy to mistake one for the other."

"Dad, I don—"

"Damn, I'd almost forgotten how amazing your cooking smells, Mrs. Baker."

You've got to be freaking kidding me. My gaze shot to the entryway, my heart steadily picking up speed. "Did you know about this?"

"I didn't. Maybe Caden invited him along." Dad's chuckle filled the air. "This reminds me of when you were still kids. I swear, some days I wondered if that boy even had a home. Not that I minded having him over."

Yeah, he'd been a damn constant in our lives up until the moment he wasn't.

Since my stupid emotions were all over the freaking place, I felt another sting behind my eyes as my brain provided me with the memory of the one—and only—night I'd spent with Gage Calloway.

The silly naïve girl I'd been had wanted to believe it'd meant as much to him as it had to me. I'd fallen asleep in his arms dreaming and wishing that I was going to wake up and things were going to be different.

Because after years and years of pining over my brother's best friend he finally saw *me*.

How stupid I'd been.

When I woke up, things were different all right. Gage hadn't just left me alone in bed, he'd gotten the hell out of town. Taking my broken heart with him.

Shoving the memory and the tears away, I squared my shoulders and said, "I can't stay." I barely managed one step when my dad caught me by the wrist.

"I'm sure the reason for your anger toward him is one-hundred percent validated," he said tugging me closer. "And I would never put you in an uncomfortable spot on purpose but I'm asking you to stay. Not for him but for me and your mom."

"Dad, I—"

The rest of the words died on my tongue the instant I spotted Gage trailing behind my mom and brother. And not because he looked all kinds of sinful in dark jeans and a black tee stretched so tight over his arms and chest it might as well have been painted on.

Nope, it was because of the girl walking beside him.

The town's rumor mill had been going on about Gage and his daughter since he moved back. And since I'd been actively avoiding running into him, I had no idea if she really existed.

If I were being completely honest, I didn't make the effort to confirm these rumors either. Because if it had been true that would've meant I had to concede that Gage had good in him.

And I really, really didn't want to do that.

It was easier to believe he was a selfish prick with no heart than the alternative. The one where he left because of me and not because of his lack of morals.

"Look who stopped by," my mom chirped.

My gaze shifted from my mom to my brother—who pulled his shoulders to his ears—before finally landing on Gage. Much to my surprise, those green eyes were already focused on me. Studying me so closely, I felt the intensity of his stare low, low in my belly.

I had this sudden urge to stomp over to where he was standing and demand he tell why he was looking at me like that. Like I was something he craved. Didn't he know he had no right?

No damn right.

"I don't believe you've met Maia yet?" he said in that low smooth voice I hated.

Happy to be looking anywhere else, my eyes flicked to the girl in question. Eyes trained on the floor and hugging a book close to her chest, she looked withdrawn and maybe a bit uncomfortable.

I couldn't blame her. Being the new girl in town definitely didn't come with any perks. If people weren't staring, they were probably whispering or asking personal questions. Poor girl probably felt like a fish out of water.

At least she wouldn't have to worry about me or my family. Us Bakers had never needed to pry…unless it was absolutely necessary of course.

"I'm so hungry, I could eat an entire cow right now," Caden groaned as he pushed into the kitchen and headed straight for the stove.

"Please don't." Our mom was right on his heel, giving his hand a smack when he attempted to lift the lid on the pasta pan.

Because I was still so focused on Gage and his daughter, I didn't miss the way her eyes shot to Caden and my mom or the small upward curve of her lips.

At least my family was entertaining I thought just as my dad squeezed my shoulder, wordlessly urging me to go introduce myself. Which wouldn't have been a problem if Gage wasn't standing there.

I didn't want him in space and sure as shit didn't want to be in his.

But I also didn't want this poor innocent girl to think she wasn't worth talking to. So I pulled up my big girl panties and walked over to where they were standing.

Lifting my lips into a smile, I held out my hand. "Nice to meet you, Maia. I'm Frankie."

I was a bit confused when instead of immediately taking my hand, she turned her questioning gaze to Gage. "That's boy's name," she not-so-subtly whispered.

I wanted to laugh, but it got stuck in my throat when Gage's eyes met mine before he oh-so-lovingly put his arm around her shoulder and whispered something next to her ear.

If that wasn't enough to make my ovaries tingle, he just had to press a fatherly kiss to her temple, effectively sending my poor lady bits into orbit. Ugh! Why did this man have to have such a nice side to him?

And why in the name of all things holy did it make me want to climb him like a tree? Or possibly rub myself all over him like an attention-seeking cat.

"Sorry. Hi."

At the soft voice, I quickly blinked out of my stupor. While I'd been lost who knew where Maia had finally touched her palm to mine. I couldn't help but smile even wider at the young girl because behind all the uncertainty burning in her golden irises, I saw curiosity too.

After a quick shake, she pulled her hand back and tucked the book she'd been holding closer to her chest. "Nice to meet you too."

"What do—"

"Come on, Maia, help me set the table on the patio."

Caden and I spoke in tandem. Clearly comfortable with him, Maia followed my brother out without hesitation. My mom and dad behind them barely a minute later.

Which left me and Gage awkwardly hovering just inside the entrance of the kitchen. "So…uh…we better go eat. Mom doesn't like waiting."

"I still remember, Frankie." He held my gaze, those eyes so serious and intense I almost believed he was talking about something other than my mom and her lack of patience when it came to food.

A gentle shiver danced its way along my skin leaving a trail of goosebumps in its wake. For years and years, I'd wondered if he remembered that night as vividly as I had. As I still did. Pain, very unwelcome pain, shot through my body like hot daggers. Anger shortly on its heels.

Although this time I was angry at myself for allowing a memory that should've been dead and forgotten to affect me like this. But that was the thing with these little life-changing moments in time; they would always be there.

Lurking in the darkest recesses of your mind. Patiently waiting for the opportune time to strike. The target? Your heart. Always your heart.

And mine had taken about enough battering as it could handle for one day.

Without saying another word, I pushed past Gage and rushed to the patio. "Mom, Dad, I'm really sorry but I have to go. I promise we'll do dinner later in the week, okay?"

I must've been pretty shit at hiding my frazzled emotions because after giving me one look neither of them even attempted to ask me to stay. Moving as fast as I could, I gave both my parents a peck on the cheek and a half-assed wave to Maia and Caden before rushing out the door.

I'd barely cleared the last porch step when long, strong fingers curled around my wrist. "Frankie." Using the arm he was holding as a lever, Gage tugged until I spun around to face him.

He was so close I could see the vein in his neck strumming out a wild beat. Behind my ribs, my heart was doing something similar. "Don't go. The last thing I want to do is chase you out of your parents' home."

"Don't flatter yourself."

"Drop the bravado." He lowered his head, looking me directly in the eye when he spoke, "You're upset."

"Yeah, no shit, Sherlock."

I was expecting him to give me one of his signature comebacks. Instead, his brows drew together while his eyes searched mine. A myriad of emotions dancing in those green depths, but I recognized only one.

Regret.

The impact of it made me feel dizzy, almost like I couldn't breathe. Using my free hand, I dragged my palm over my collarbone and curled my fingers over my shoulder, the tips desperately digging into my skin.

"I can't do this," I mumbled under my breath. "Not now…Not—"

Before I had time to finish the rest of my sentence or even react, he hooked his hand around my neck and pulled my face closer. So freaking close that I could feel the warmth of his breath flutter over my lips.

The need to close my eyes and inhale him was so strong, it scared the shit out of me. I felt completely off-balance, like I was standing on the edge of a cliff. One wrong move or too-strong breeze and I'd tumble over.

"Frankie," he breathed, sounding broken and desperate. "Please, talk to me." My heart slammed to an abrupt stop before picking up again at twice the speed. My brain producing questions faster than I could think.

What's there to talk about?

Why now?

Why are you doing this?

White-hot fire filled my lungs with the effort it took to keep myself from cussing and yelling. At him. At the universe. At myself.

I had to get some sense of control back. Some sense of normal. And I had to do it far, far away from Gage Calloway.

"Just let me leave." The words fell from my lips, angry and cold. Shocking me when the taste of it left guilt lingering on my tongue. Didn't I have a right to be furious with this man? To hate him with every fiber of my being?

Suddenly, I wasn't so sure.

Anger and confusion were still warring inside of me when Gage's hand slipped from my neck and he took two wide steps backward.

"Have a good night, Frankie."

He gave me one long meaningful look that just about incinerated my insides before turning on his heel and making his way back inside my parents' house.

What the hell just happened?

Too tired to figure anything out, I hopped in my car and drove to Maddie's place. I'd barely rolled to a stop in her driveway when I saw her and Adam beyond the kitchen window. They were either cooking or cleaning up, whatever it was they looked happy.

Maddie's smile was huge as she shook her head furiously. A second later, Adam grabbed her face and kissed her. That stupid organ behind my ribs twisted and squeezed to the point of pain, cruelly reminding me of everything I wanted but didn't have.

With a sharp shake of my head, I threw my car in reverse and got the hell out of there. Only to be mocked by the silence that greeted me when I walked through my front door.

"This is ridiculous," I huffed out as I flopped down onto the couch. An obnoxiously loud groan pushed past my lips as I threw my head back and stared at the ceiling. Then it hit me.

Jumping up, I shoved my hands into my front pockets. A second later, I had my new phone in one hand and a business card in the other. I dragged my thumb over the name on the card a few times before I blew out a breath and started typing.

Me: ***Hey, it's Frankie. Let's do dinner next week Wednesday. 8 pm at Olive and Vine? Can't wait to see you.***

That last part was a lie, but nobody needed to know that.

9

GAGE

You're sure? I need you to be sure, Frankie."

Eyes so blue they rivaled the stunning color of the ocean on a cloudless day peered up at me from beneath thick lashes. Sinking her teeth into her bottom lip—still swollen from my kiss—she blinked once, twice before slowly walking backward out of my reach.

Flicking my tongue out, I stole a taste of her off my own lips while my gaze stayed glued to her fingers slowly undoing the buttons of her blue sundress.

My skin, my pants, everything, *felt too damn tight.*

"I've wanted this from the moment I saw you as more than just my brother's friend." Without breaking eye contact, Frankie shrugged out of the now unbuttoned dress. I sucked in a ragged breath and immediately had to do it again.

Because shit, she was beautiful.

Standing before me in nothing but the skin she was born in with the soft light of the moon almost caressing her curves, she was the most beautiful thing I'd ever seen, and I didn't feel worthy.

"I want you, Gage."

My eyes flew open as I furiously tried to catch my breath. I'd been having this dream—or rather reliving this memory—more times than I could count over the last couple of months. And I always woke up right after she admitted to wanting me.

Maybe it was because I wanted those words to be true here in our present and not just our past?

I shook my head and shoved fingers through my hair. The tips scraping my scalp as I stared at the ceiling. It didn't take long for images of Frankie to cloud my vision. Tiny snaps of everything leading up to that night on the beach and then every dreadful thing after, finally ending with the look on her face outside her parents' house a few nights ago.

I squeezed my eyes shut against the vision, but it was no use. For as long as I lived, I would never be able to forget that look. Unfiltered anguish had shone so bright in her eyes, it nearly crippled me.

I wasn't stupid enough to believe she wasn't angry with me. Hell, she had every right to be. I just wasn't prepared for her hurt to outshine her fury.

Hurt I'd put there.

"Shiiit." I scrubbed my palm down my face and cursed some more. "Shit, shit, shit." How in the name of all things holy did I end up hurting the one woman who'd meant the world to me for far longer than she even realized?

And more importantly, how the fuck was I going to make it right?

Blowing out a breath through my nose, I turned my head toward the window. Through the small slits in the blinds, I could see it wasn't dark, but it wasn't light either. I twisted on my side and a quick tap against my phone's screen confirmed that trying to sleep now would be utterly useless since my alarm would be shrieking to life within the next thirty minutes.

Might as well get up and get on with the day.

I shoved the covers aside before slipping from the bed and ambling toward the en suite bathroom, turning on the shower moment I stepped inside. It didn't take long for the water to reach optimal temperature and I couldn't stop the groan from pushing past my lips when the warm spray rained down over my skin.

It felt so damn good.

The only thing that could've possibly made it any better was if Frankie was in there with me. Now, I knew these kinds of thoughts usually landed me in a rather hard situation. Trouble was once my mind went down that path, it turned into a freight train with no stop in sight.

I imagined her standing before me, smile wide, and her body beautifully naked with those inky strands spilling over her shoulders and covering her breasts. The image of Frankie was so clear, I could almost reach out and gently brush her hair out of the way. Or even better, lower my head to her breast and suck the tip into my mouth.

I swear, the fantasy was so vivid; I could just about taste her on my tongue.

Splaying one hand on the tiles in front of me, I rolled my neck and dropped my chin to my chest. I screwed my eyes shut, my free hand sliding down my abs. Lower and lower until my fist closed around my throbbing hard-on. Squeezing once, I slowly slid my hand up and down, still so very lost in all things Frankie.

Behind my closed lids, images of her played out like a movie before me. I could see the saucy smile on her face as she dropped to her knees and wrapped those pretty lips around me. Would she take me deep or just tease until I fisted her hair and plundered her mouth like a damn beast?

Groaning, my hand worked faster as the fantasy inside my head continued to build.

In this image, it was *me* on *my* knees with my face buried between her thighs. Licking and sucking on that sweet spot while she chanted my name like a prayer and begged for more.

Which I'd happily give her until neither of us could damn well walk.

I was so far gone, my movements became fast and choppy and my world finally exploded with Frankie's name rolling off my tongue in a hoarse whisper.

"Fuck," I groaned as I dropped my forehead to the tiles and heaved out a breath. Was this what my life had come to? Jerking off in the shower to the memory of a woman who couldn't stand the sight of me?

With a sharp shake of my head, I cleaned myself up and got dressed. Ten minutes later, I was standing in the kitchen willing the slow drip of the coffee to hurry the hell up. Maybe some caffeine in my system would drown out all things Frankie? Because I needed a damn reprieve.

If I wasn't thinking about every little thing I desperately wanted to do to her naked body, my mind was conjuring up the image of her eyes filled with pain. I would've done just about anything to remove that picture from my brain. But I guessed living with the knowledge of how deeply I'd hurt her was my just reward for the way I'd acted those years ago.

Forcing the thoughts away, I grabbed a mug from the cabinet just as Maia shuffled into the kitchen.

"Morning, Dad," she mumbled around a yawn, wiping the sleep from her eyes.

I topped up my mug before spinning around to face her. “Good morning. Did you have a good sleep?”

Dragging her feet to the fridge, she mumbled something under her breath before she pulled out an apple juice and settled on one of the stools at the breakfast nook.

“What’s for breakfast?”

I shrugged. “Not sure yet. What are you in the mood for?”

Maia grinned like she’d just want the lottery. “Can I pick anything I want?”

“I know what’s going on in that head of yours.” I leaned forward and narrowed my eyes. “No, you can not have pop tarts for breakfast.”

“Ugh, fiiiine. I guess toast will do.”

Shaking my head on a laugh, I popped two slices of bread in the toaster before I took a long swallow of coffee before setting the mug on the counter and leaning my hip against it. “I have a shift at the fire station tonight, you’ll be sleeping over at Nan’s.”

Somewhere in the back of my mind was this niggling feeling that something was bothering her. It could very well have been because we still needed to settle and find our new normal or it could have been something bigger.

“I know we’ve talked about this before but if me volunteering at the station is too much right now, you know you can tell me, right?”

From the moment moving back to Clearwater Bay had been on the table, Maia and I had discussed what it would mean for us. I’d told her about firefighting and how desperately I’d wanted to get back into it.

We’d talked about the risks and the horrible hours. I’d been so sure we could make it all work. Now I wasn’t so sure. In the week we'd been back she'd already spent two nights at Nan's.

If I ever got offered a permanent position, she'd have to spend way more than two nights a week away from home.

Shit! I was beginning to think I was doing the parenting thing wrong.

"It's not that, Dad."

"Then what? Talk to me?"

Maia's nose scrunched up in a way that made my heart squeeze. "It's this school."

Pushing off the counter, I slipped onto the stool next to her and draped my arm over her shoulders. "Hey, I know it's all new and strange right now, but it will get better."

Maia bent her head, her long dark hair falling over the side of her face like a curtain. One I was certain she wanted to hide behind. Brushing the locks away from her face, I nudged her shoulder with mine until we made eye contact in a sideways glance.

"It *will* get better," I said again.

Maia shifted her attention to the bottle of apple juice in front of her. "I don't fit in." If she'd spoken any softer, I wouldn't have heard her. But I had and shit if it didn't have my damn heart breaking in two.

I wasn't remotely prepared for this. Not even a little. "Maia." I reached for her stool and swiveled it until she had no other choice than to face me. "I'm not going to sit here and tell you school isn't hard. Because it is. It's so fucking hard. Kids say and do things without giving it a second thought or even considering the consequences."

"And I know, boy do I know, how much worse it is in a small town like this. Getting up and showing up takes courage. And you do that every day without fail, Maia. It might feel like you don't fit in but that's only because you were born to stand out."

Even as her eyes shone bright with tears, her lips twitched. "You dropped an f-bomb. Nan is going to love that."

Pursing my lips, I cocked a brow. "Really that's all you got from my *wonderful* speech?"

I barely had time to brace myself before Maia was out of her stool, launching herself at me. Arms wrapped tightly around my neck, she sniffled into my shoulder. "Love you, Dad."

When she pulled away and I got a glimpse of her face, the relief I'd felt moments ago dissolved to nothingness. Those brows were still pinched tight and the weight of the world still sitting heavy on her shoulders.

"Anything else eating you?"

She swallowed hard and started shaking her head. I laid my hand on her arm and gently reminded her, "No secrets, remember?" When Maia and I became a family, it was the one thing we promised each other; no secrets. Ever. It didn't matter how big or bad the situation was, we'd always face it together.

Blowing out a breath way too heavy for a kid her age, she pulled her shoulders into a shrug. "I've just been thinking."

"About?" I nudged.

"Did…did you let Mrs. Reiner know we moved here?"

"Why would you be thinking about that?" I had an inkling what the answer would be, but I hoped to all things holy I was wrong.

Maia nibbled her lip, her cheeks turning rosy. "I…" she huffed out a loaded breath sending a few strands of her hair flying. "I want my mom to have my address in case she wants to write or something."

I took a silent steady breath through my nose and held it for three seconds before releasing it in the same manner. Maia's caseworker had tried her best to prepare me. She'd given me enough reading material to last a damn lifetime, and it still wasn't enough.

Because how the hell was I supposed to tell my daughter that the woman who gave birth to her cared more about sticking a damn needle into her arm than her own flesh and blood? That she'd given up her right to be a parent without putting a single thought behind it.

No, I could never break *my* kid's heart like that.

My hand found hers and squeezed. "Mrs. Reiner knows, but baby, I gotta ask you to not dig, okay?" She opened her mouth, and I silenced her with a sharp shake of my head. "Mrs. Reiner said it would be best if you don't have contact with your mom for a while. She needs to get better and so do you."

She pursed her lips, the little muscle in her cheek jumping a mile a minute. "Okay."

"I'm serious about this," I said firmly.

"All right. I said I wouldn't." she snatched her hand away. "Can I get dressed now?"

"Be quick, we need to leave soon." My tone was short and snappy, but my anger wasn't meant for her. It was toward her mother, the system, and every other person who had done her wrong in her short life.

I just hoped like hell I didn't end up on that list too.

10

FRANKIE

"Holy hell." Leaning over the steering wheel, my nose almost touched the windshield as I tried—and failed—to take in the craziness. Vehicles and machines I had no hope of identifying littered what used to be a fairly quiet street while people with hardhats and fluorescent vests ran around like marching ants on a mission.

Guess the fire brought in some really good business for the surrounding construction companies I thought as I parked my car in a spot closest to the bakery. Instead of getting out, I sat back and took everything in once again.

It was unnerving how fast things could change. One moment we're opening and closing our shops and the next we're desperately trying to salvage them. Not that there was anything for Mr. Hamilton to salvage.

I let out a breath, my gaze traveling to the spot down the street where the dry cleaner used to be. It had been a constant in our little town for as long as I could remember. And now it was nothing more than a pile of rubble.

My heart squeezed tight. As far as I knew, the dry cleaner was the only thing Mr. Hamilton had. He'd never gotten married or had any kids, his parents were no longer with us and he had no siblings.

Turning my attention back to the bakery, I made a mental note to stop by Mr. Hamilton's place to see how he was doing. I was pretty sure he could use a friendly face and maybe a cupcake or two.

Once that was settled, I climbed out of my car. After grabbing the container from my passenger seat, I sucked in a fortifying breath and headed inside. I'd barely set foot on-site before the devil himself—aka Gage—came rushing toward me.

Hands furiously waving, he motioned for me to stop. As much as I wanted to ignore the asshole, I couldn't. When Caden had called me earlier in the morning, he'd made it abundantly clear that Gage was in charge and I had to use my listening ears whenever I was on site.

It was because of that, and *only* that, I forced my feet to stop moving when all I really wanted to do was turn around and get the hell away from the man approaching me. And not even because of the deep-rooted hate I felt for him—which I wasn't entirely sure I felt anymore—but rather the insane dreams I'd had because of him.

If the twenty-year-old version of him wasn't seducing me and breaking my heart, the older, gruffer one held me against his chest and whispered sweet nothings in my ear. Yeah, I'd had a pretty shitty sleep thanks to all of that rolling around inside my head like a damn tumbleweed.

And I blamed Gage for it all.

"Looking fine this morning, Baker."

I barely resisted the urge to roll my eyes. Though in all fairness, I wasn't sure if it was at him or the delicious shiver dancing down my spine at the sound of his gritty timbre. "What do you want?"

His eyes roved over my body. Slowly, steadily taking me in from head to toe. What did he see? Was it still that naïve girl he'd taken for a fool or something else entirely? As much as I would have liked to know the answer, I wasn't about to give him the satisfaction of asking it.

"Last time I checked; my eyes were up here," I snapped.

Instead of immediately lifting his gaze to meet mine, those eyes of his leisurely swept up my body, pausing at my breasts. Tilting his head slightly, his brows pinched together as he studied my boobs like they were some foreign object.

I wasn't too pissed because I knew what he was looking at. I'd chosen to wear my favorite shirt today. It was the brightest, happiest yellow and had two bees with ghost heads on it exactly where my boobs were. Just below in cursive font, it said *boo bees.*

I knew the moment it clicked, that stupid sinful mouth of his quirked upward, his dimple popping deliciously. I wanted to smack it off his ridiculously hot face and then kiss it better afterward.

Wait, what?

I blinked the stupid thought away, Gage's sparkling green eyes instantly coming into focus. "I have to admit," he said all low and gritty. "those *boo bees* sure look inviting."

"Ugh." This time I ignored the insistent tug low in my belly and rolled my eyes. "Did you actually want something, or did you just stop me to be a douche?"

Taking a step forward, he splayed his big hand over his chest. "Ouch, you're breaking my heart here."

"Please, you'd have to have a heart for it to be able to break." My annoying brain chose that moment to remind me he'd adopted a girl and loved her as his own, so he probably had a big, beautiful heart.

Just not when it came to me.

Irritated with myself, I huffed out, "Seriously Gage, what do you want?"

His features went from playful to serious within the space of a breath. Those impossibly lush lips parted for a second before he snapped them shut again. Brows pulled together, I stared at him as he shook his head and chuckled. Although it didn't sound remotely joyous.

"You can't come in here," he finally said.

Tilting my chin upward, I pulled my shoulders back. "The hell I can't. This is my damn bakery."

"You didn't let me finish." Gage spread his legs and crossed his arms in front of him. The action drew my attention to his thick biceps and the way the muscles popped so deliciously. I want to wrap my hands around it and squeeze just to feel the hardness jump beneath my fingertips.

Wait…am I still thinking about his biceps or something else?

Before I could answer myself—as one does—Gage cleared his throat a little too loud. I dragged my eyes away from his arms to meet his gaze. I fully expected to see amusement dance behind those green irises so when they shimmered with unmistakable heat, my legs almost gave out.

He was looking at me like he wanted to do the dirtiest things and I wasn't entirely sure how I felt about it. My lady bits, on the other hand, they were singing and clapping, practically begging the man to do whatever he wanted to.

Ugh! I really need to get laid.

That was the only explanation I had for whatever the hell was going on. Because if I was in my right mind—and completely satiated—there would be no way I would be thinking about Gage and those big hands and all the places I wanted to feel them.

"Yo, bossman," I heard someone yell. "Can I borrow you for a sec?"

Brows knitted together; Gage blinked a few times. Without taking his eyes off me, he flung his hand, index finger pointing skyward, in the direction the voice had come from. "Be right there."

Then he took two steps forward, invading my space and lighting up my senses. "You need protection." His voice, low and gravelly rolled over my skin teasing my nerve endings, setting my pulse on fire.

I licked my suddenly dry lips, his gaze zeroing in on the action with superhuman speed. "Why exactly do I need protection?"

His eyes slowly traveled back up to meet mine. I wasn't sure why but I held my breath, anxiously waiting. For what exactly I didn't know.

"This is a working site; you need protective gear before you can be on the premises." He leaned forward a little, those lips of his close enough nibble on. "You could get hurt."

"That so?" My eyebrow climbed toward my hairline. "Some might argue I'd already gotten hurt."

"Frankie."

I held up my hand, I didn't really want to do this, I just liked being petty sometimes. "I get it; no safety gear, no entry." I pulled the container out from under my arm and shoved it in his direction. "I just wanted to drop these off for the guys. Show my appreciation and all that."

"What's this?" he asked as he took the container from me. His calloused hand scraped over the back of my fingers during the transfer and I bit my tongue to stop myself from cussing out loud.

When my hands were finally free, I shoved them into my back pockets, hoping like hell the tingling feeling coating my skin would disappear soon. "It's an assortment of muffins. Some savory, some sweet." I shrugged. "Figured the guys might like a snack."

"Muffins huh?" Not caring that I was right there in front of him, he removed the lid and lifted the container to his nose before inhaling deeply. "Mmm, can't wait to get my mouth on your muffin."

It didn't matter how he meant it, my poor sex-deprived brain only provided me with images of him kneeling before me. Hands threaded through his hair, that sinful mouth driving me insane while he provided me with enough pleasure to make my toes curl.

Oh for shit's sake! This was Gage. I seriously needed to get a damn grip. Preferably a penis-sized one with a man who wasn't Gage attached to it. Slicking my tongue over my teeth, I gave him a piss-off stare. "Dream on! Your filthy mouth isn't coming anywhere near my muffin."

It didn't have the desired effect. Being the asshole he was, Gage stared right back at me, the intensity in his eyes flooding me with heat. So much heat. That turned into a raging inferno when he ignored my personal bubble and inched closer still.

Gaze bouncing between my eyes and my lips, he murmured, "You sure about that? I bet you'd feel *so good* watching me devour every bit of it. You'd probably even beg me to eat it again."

Shit! I was fairly certain we hadn't been talking about food at all and one-hundred percent sure I was turned-on beyond belief and now needed a change of underwear. He didn't need to know any of this. Although if he chanced a look at my chest, I was pretty sure my *boo bees* would be dead giveaways.

Lifting my chin higher, I said, "You're awfully full of yourself."

"You could be full of me too."

"What?"

"Calloway!"

One of the workers and I spoke at the same time.

"Gotta go." Jogging backward, he hefted the container high. The stupid grin on his lips bringing out those knee-weakening dimples. "Thanks for these." Then he spun around and disappeared from view.

I stood rooted to the spot for who knew how long before I spun around and stomped to my car. Mumbling an array of, "stupid cocksucker, dickwad, asshole," as I went. Safely tucked behind the steering wheel of my car, I heaved out a breath and dropped my chin to my chest.

One look at my *boo bees* and I was cussing again. Turning the key, I shoved the car into gear. As I pulled away from the curb and headed home, I wondered if I had enough time to take my *rabbit* for a quick spin before Misty arrived.

11

FRANKIE

"Geez, you're squeezing the life out that poor piping bag."

I closed my eyes and pulled in a long ass breath through my nose before slowly releasing it. Dropping the bag in question to the counter, my fingers found my temples, moving in small, steady circles.

It really wasn't Misty's fault I was in a mood. Even though the particular high pitch of her voice didn't help matters much. Still, my current state had nothing to do with her. Nope, this was all sexual frustration and anger.

Not the best mix.

Especially since my body couldn't decide which emotion to go with. One moment I was all hot and bothered, in desperate need of an orgasm, and the next I wanted to punch something—or someone—repeatedly.

Yeah, this was no fun at all.

"I know this situation must be so bad for you," Misty said completely unaware of the war raging inside of me. "But we'll be back at Sugar Booger before you know it. I mean, seriously, you have your brother working on it. And he's the best."

She snatched one of the empty frosting bowls off the counter and moved to the sink to wash it. "And that other guy too. What's his name again?" Misty's head angled to the side.

"Gage," I provided dryly.

"Yes!" she squealed. "That's the one. Oh and isn't he sooo yummy? I mean, your brother is too, but this Gage guy just oozes sex."

Good thing Misty's back was to me; within the space of a breath my stare turned to daggers directly aimed at her. Poor girl, all she did was mention how hot Gage was—an extremely accurate statement—and suddenly my claws were out, ready to scratch.

Poor girl? A little voice in the back of my head mocked. *Poor you for still being hung up on the guy.*

This freeloading bitch seriously needed a lesson in shut the hell up. And possibly one in mind your damn business too.

I bit my lip to keep myself from laughing. Because if anyone knew about the things, the conversations, going on inside my head, they'd lock me up and throw away the key.

They probably should still do that.

"So what do you think?" Misty's high-pitched voice pulled me back from crazy town.

Brows furrowed, I picked up my discarded piping bag and swirled a good amount of chocolate frosting onto the waiting orange-rind cupcake. "You might want to say that again, I kinda spaced out."

A shrill sound that was meant to be a giggle filled my not-so-tiny kitchen. I barely resisted the urge to slap my hands over my ears. Again, it wasn't her fault I was this on edge and irritated.

On any normal day, I could handle Misty's ear-splitting vocals. Hell, some days I found it endearing. Today though, it felt a lot like nails scraping on a chalkboard. Even more so when I heard the words tumbling out of her mouth.

"I said," she drawled, "I'd would really like to ask Gage out for a coffee or maybe even dinner. I know I don't normally do things so forward, but…" she trailed off.

For reasons I couldn't fathom, I wanted to grab her by the shoulders and shake her while demanding she stay away from Gage. To tell her he wasn't hers.

Shit! He wasn't mine either.

This sudden all-consuming possessiveness was as new as it was unwanted. I couldn't and shouldn't give two shits who Gage wanted to share his bed with. It wasn't my business.

It had never been my business.

Yet, here I was desperately trying to calm the rage that had no permission to be inside me.

"Yeah," I croaked out. "You…uh…yeah." Closing my eyes, I sucked in a breath and told myself to get over whatever the hell was going on. When I opened them again, every word I spoke dripped with resolve, "You should totally do that."

Suddenly overcome with the need to be alone, I set the piping bag back down and walked over to the containers already stacked with treats. "Why don't you take these over to Morning Kick I'm sure Susan is not-so-patiently waiting for them. Then you can take the rest of the day."

Misty's brows pulled together. "Are you okay? Did I say something wrong?" Despite her looking a bit ditzy, she was anything but. It was one of the reasons why I hired her. She was sharp. Maybe a little too sharp right now.

"You didn't do anything." In all honesty, she really hadn't. She was single. So was Gage. If she wanted to ask him out on a date, she had every damn right to do so. My stupid, stupid heart just needed to understand that.

I pushed the stack of containers toward her. "I'm just feeling a bit…off. And I'm afraid I'll be horrible company today. Besides when I'm done with that batch," I motioned toward the tray of unfrosted cupcakes, "I'm done for the day too."

Uncertainty coated every syllable she spoke. "You're sure?"

"Hundred percent."

"Well, all right then." Misty grabbed her bag and the stacked containers. "See you tomorrow."

All I could muster was a smile and nod. I waited until I could no longer hear her car before I let out the breath I'd been holding. Smacking my palms down on the smooth, cold marble, I bowed my head. "Screw you, Gage Callaway. Screw you very much."

I would have loved to say it to his face, but I wasn't stupid enough to believe I could talk to him right that second and not be affected. What I needed was to talk this through with the one person who knew me better than I knew myself.

That was why I found myself driving to Maddie's dance studio not even 20 minutes later. With another container of cupcakes and cinnamon rolls safely strapped in my passenger seat, of course.

Treats in hand, I walked through the doors of SoulBeat a few minutes later. A smile immediately touching my lips when I found Maddie twirling and spinning on the floor to a Christina Perri song.

Whenever I saw her in her element like that, unfiltered happiness washed over me. Because I knew how hard she'd had to fight for her dreams. She didn't know this, but I looked up to her in so many ways.

She was strong in places where I was weak. I'd seen it in the way she'd been with her fiancé, Adam in the very beginning. And in the way she kept dreaming even on the days when all hope was gone.

Still unaware of my presence, she jumped through the air, legs stretched out, arms reaching for the sky. The moment her feet touched the floor, she curled forward. Her head almost touching her feet. Slowly she began to straighten while spinning around and around.

Watching her dance like this was enough to steal the breath from my lungs.

Maddie was mid-turn when she finally spotted me. Losing her balance slightly, she clutched at her chest. "You scared the crap out of me." She eyed the door then me again. "I thought I'd locked that."

"Nope. You definitely didn't." I held up the containers in my hand. "I brought treats."

I almost laughed when Maddie clapped her hands together, looking as excited as a teenage girl seeing her crush. I supposed baked goods sometimes did that to people, so I couldn't hold it against her too much.

After grabbing a towel, Maddie rushed over to where I was standing. Smile all big and bright. "What yumminess are you spoiling me with today?"

I held out the containers for her. "Cupcakes and cinnamon rolls."

She snatched them from me in the same way a starved person would grab a bowl of soup on a rainy day. "Mmm," she moaned when she lifted one of the lids. "Smells so good." With a quick jerk of her head, she motioned for me to follow her to her office.

As we trudged along, my gaze bounced from wall to wall. Grinning as I took in the repainted walls and fancy new fixtures. I had been here when most of these renovations were done and I still couldn't believe it was Maddie's dad who had done it.

Unlike my relationship with my parents—which reminded me I needed to answer my mom's worried text from the previous night—Maddie's one with hers had been turbulent at best.

Until a while ago when everything took a sudden change for the better. Or maybe it hadn't been so sudden since I knew Maddie was still healing and I guessed her parents were too.

I couldn't imagine living like that—another reason I admired her so fiercely. The cruel words they'd sometimes thrown at her or the times I'd hated them on her behalf, didn't matter. Not to her. She'd still loved them unconditionally even when she'd been walking around with a hole inside her heart.

"All right," Maddie sing-songed when we entered her office, effectively pulling me back to the present. "Are you gonna tell me what's eating you or am I going to have to shake it out of ya?"

And this was why she was my best friend.

Taking my hand, Maddie led me to the couch below the two-way mirror that looked out onto the studio floor. After we plonked down and tucked our legs under us, she leaned back and waited.

I looked everywhere except her before I finally said, "I think Gage is messing with my head."

"Why?" Her tone was careful, measured. I'd known her long enough to know this didn't mean she was calm at all.

"I don't know how to explain it." Sighing heavily, I pulled my braid over my shoulder and rubbed the elastic holding my hair together between thumb and index finger.

"We've been having these weird moments where everything we say is inadvertently about sex. And maybe it's just been a while, but shit, almost every encounter has left me feeling all sorts of hot."

Her eyes narrowed. "Uh huh."

Ignoring her tone, I babbled on, "And then there was that freaking weird moment at my parents' place the other night. I thought for sure he was going to kiss me."

"What moment now?"

I rubbed my hand over my face before I launched into everything that'd happened between Gage and me. Once the word vomit started, it showed no sign of letting up. I talked and talked and talked. Finally ending with, "I mean he can't be that big of an asshole if he was willing to take in a complete stranger and raise her as his own."

Maddie pursed her lips. "A leopard never changes its spots. Do I need to remind you that you woke up naked in a tent…alone?"

I ground my teeth at the memory. So vivid, I could still feel the breeze wash over my skin. Could still feel my heart shatter into tiny pieces the moment I realized I was the only one there.

"No, Maddie-Cakes, you don't."

She put her hand on my leg, giving it a reassuring squeeze. "I'm sorry, I don't mean to pick at old wounds. It's just…I'm still so angry about it all. I don't care how long ago it all happened, I can *never* forgive him for it."

I couldn't help but chuckle. "Shouldn't I be the angry one here?"

"Yes! Yes, you should." She swiped a hand through the air. "I'd lost my friend for the longest time after that day. I'd thought I'd never get you back. Because he took something, that special something that had made you *you*."

It was easy to forget how one tiny moment in time could affect so many people. And yeah, maybe it was part of being young and stupid. Maybe it was a lesson in trust. I didn't know exactly.

But for eighteen-year-old me offering up my virginity had been a big deal. Naïve is it may have been, I'd dreamt of forever with that boy. And in one cruel move, he'd ripped that dream from my heart, leaving a gaping wound in its place.

For years I'd hated him for it.

Now, I wasn't sure what I felt. I just knew it wasn't hate anymore.

Maddie squeezed my leg again, the action drawing my gaze to hers. "How I feel about Gage really doesn't matter. If I'd taken what other people thought into account," she gave me a pointed stare, "you included, Adam and I would have never been."

She had a point there. I wasn't the biggest fan of her making nice with the grumpy asshole next door. Especially after the way he'd treated her when they met. But she'd seen something in him that called to her soul.

I still wasn't sure if there was something more going on with these exchanges between me and Gage or if it was just a matter of SSF (seriously sexually frustrated). And honestly, I didn't want to think about it anymore. My head hurt and who the hell knew what was going on with my heart.

Lunging forward, I wrapped my friend up in the tightest hug before pulling away. With my hands perched on her shoulders, I gave her a smile I hoped conveyed everything I couldn't voice.

Giving her a gentle squeeze, I sat back and said, "Okay, enough about me. I want to hear all about these wedding ideas."

Before I knew it, the hours bled into each other and it was time for one of Maddie's classes. Our heads were still thrown back in laughter at something silly from our teenage years when the door opened, and a few elderly ladies filed in.

Maddie's eyes lit up with pure happiness and I was yet again reminded of how wrong the saying 'those who can't, teach' was. Because Maddie sure as shit could dance like the best of them but she freaking shined when she was teaching.

"Goodness," she said, pushing onto her feet. "Where did the time go?"

I shrugged, getting to my feet too. "You know what they say about it flying when you're having fun."

"Rude if you ask me."

I flicked my arm, turning my hand palm up. "I know, right?"

Maddie tried very hard to keep her features unmoving. It lasted two full seconds before she threw her head back and laughed. "Gosh, I miss this. Why aren't we doing it as much as we used to?"

Rolling my eyes with mock-annoyance, I sighed dramatically. "Well, maybe because you went and fell in love and now have something," I coughed into my hand while saying, "*someone* better to do." And then quickly added, "Which I am very happy about by the way. You were getting a bit needy."

When she didn't look convinced, I stepped forward and hugged her again. "Stop. I'm so happy you found someone, Maddie-Cakes. You deserve it."

Her eyes glittered with unshed tears when she pulled back. "What are you going to do about Gage?"

"Honestly, I have no clue." I scratched a spot above my temple. "I'm still convinced it's the lack of any action between my sheets that's messing with my brain." Waggling my brows, I said, "Maybe Brian will fix that for me after our date."

With a sharp shake of her head, Maddie laughed as she turned and headed for the door, mumbling something about not wanting to hear about it under her breath.

I had every intention of following her and quietly disappearing before the ladies started with their jazzercise until I heard someone call my name. Looking to my right, I saw Mrs. Calloway push through the small elderly crowd and hurry toward me.

Great. As much as I adored her, I really wasn't in a mood to make small talk with Gage's grandma. Even if she was just as batty as me. But because of those pesky manners my mom had drilled into me, I smiled and met her halfway.

"Hi, Mrs. Calloway. Haven't seen you in a while. How are you?" I eyed her bright pink and purple hair. "Awesome do you're rocking."

Her hands immediately found the edges of her hair, pride curving her lips upward. "Why thank you, Francesca. Mr. Howard sure seems to think so too." Her thin, gray brows happily bounced up and down.

The laugh that wanted to bubble up almost made it all the way out until I heard, "Ew, Nan," before Gage's daughter—wow, that sounded so weird—stepped out from behind Mrs. Calloway.

Her gaze collided with mine just as her grandma threw an arm over her shoulder and pulled her close. "Oh hush you. Don't tell me your father hasn't had the birds and bees talk with you yet?"

Then Mrs. Calloway beamed at me. "I don't believe you've met my granddaughter yet. This here is—"

"Maia," I finished for her.

Mrs. Calloway's features brightened even more while Maia trained her eyes on me. Those golden-brown irises burning bright with confusion. Almost like she couldn't believe I remembered her name.

Which only had me frowning in return. Even if she hadn't been Gage's daughter, she'd still be pretty damn hard to forget.

"I didn't know you two had met before," Mrs. Calloway's voice cut pulled my attention to her just in time to see her lean forward expectedly. "When exactly was this?"

"At my parents' last night," my gaze met Maia's still confused one. "But unfortunately, I had to leave early." I couldn't imagine what she must have thought or what her dad told her about me.

Just as I couldn't explain why this desperate need for her to like me suddenly sank its claws into my skin.

"All right, ladies and gentlemen, let's get jiggy," Maddie yelled from the dancefloor.

Mrs. Calloway swiveled her head to briefly look over her shoulder before turning her attention back to me. "Well, that's my cue. You won't mind keeping Maia company, will you Francesca?"

"I'm fine on my own, Nan."

"Not at all."

Maia and I spoke at the same time. Although her words came out more as a grumble.

Mrs. Calloway seemed to think we were all in agreement because she dropped a kiss to the top of Maia's head, who in turn scrunched up her nose at the public display affection, before wiggling her fingers at me in 'bye' motion.

Then she was gone leaving me alone with Maia.

"I—"

"You don't have to stay," she interrupted before I even had time to properly speak. Hugging the book she'd been clutching, closer to her chest, she hefted it higher as her chin moved closer to her chest. "I'm fine on my own."

This time though her repeated words didn't hold as much conviction as they had the first time. It gave me the impression she'd been used to people not wanting to stay. My heart broke a little right then.

How many times had I taken my parents, my life, for granted? Never giving a second thought to the fact that there were people who didn't have what I had. People who longed for just a sliver of it.

Smiling, I stepped forward and touched my palm to her forearm. When she jolted and sucked in a sharp breath, I realized my mistake and quickly pulled my hand away. Dragging in a breath of my own, I said, "I don't mind. Besides, if I leave now, I'll have to go deal with the mess in my kitchen." I leaned forward just a bit. "So, really, you're doing *me* a favor."

Maia's lips twitched like she wanted to smile but for whatever reason she refused to set it free. And I was completely okay with it because I understood she was still figuring out what to make of me. And probably wondering if she could trust me.

Making sure to keep an acceptable distance between us, I motioned toward the chairs lining the wall. "How bout we take a seat and watch the show?"

Digging her teeth into her lip, she turned her body sideways to look at the dancing seniors before eyeing the door. I was almost certain she was about to head out when she turned my way and softly said, "Okay."

Silence filled the air as we made our way to the chairs and it continued to build and stretch between us with every agonizing minute that passed. From the moment we sat down, all I wanted to do was get to know her. But I bit my tongue, knowing she needed space and hoping she'd talk to me on her own.

Naturally, I ignored the little voice in the back of my head constantly asking me why this was so important.

When I finally couldn't take it anymore, I shifted in my seat so I could face her. The book she'd held onto for dear life was now resting in her lap, her fingers slowly tracing over the colorful mandala pattern on the front.

"Are you enjoying Clearwater Bay?" I finally asked.

Pushing a few inky strands behind her ear, Maia angled her head my way and scrunched up her nose. "It's okay." She looked up, her gaze landing on the oldies swiveling their hips as she mumbled, "If you're old."

I bit the inside of my cheek to keep myself from laughing. The last thing I wanted to do was make her feel uncomfortable. "Small town living can't compare with the big city hustle, huh?"

"It's not that. It's just—" she shook her head and sucked in a breath. A long moment passed before her eyes met mine again. "Have you lived here long?"

"All my life."

"So you knew my dad when he'd still lived here?"

I grinned at her. "Yeah, we practically grew up together especially after he and Caden became attached at the hip."

Her features lit up with interest. "What was he like?"

"Your dad?" I asked and her head immediately bobbed up and down. "Oh he was a little—"

A blood curdling scream sounded from the dancefloor before I could finish my sentence. Both Maia and

I jumped up and hurried to the middle of the floor where everyone was huddling together.

Muffled moans filled my ears the closer we came, and I feared someone might've fallen down. Which was a pretty scary thought considering the entire class was well over sixty years old.

My fears were soon realized when the crowd parted to reveal Mrs. Calloway lying on her side, face contorted in agony.

12

GAGE

Heart pounding, I rushed through the doors of the emergency room. On instinct, I tuned out the chaos that met me inside and rushed toward the front desk. Just as I opened my mouth to ask about Nan, a whirlwind barreled into my side.

My hands immediately wrapped around Maia, holding her tight to me. "It's okay," I soothed. "I'm here now." I bent down to kiss the top of her head when movement in my peripheral vision had me looking to the right.

The moment my gaze landed on Frankie, I wanted to reach out and pull her to me too. That need, so powerful ran through my veins with a force that stole my breath. And it took every bit of strength I had to not act on it.

To not grab Frankie by the shoulders and shake her until she realized how desperately I needed her to be mine. But now was not the time for it. Soon though. Very, very soon her and I would have this talk.

Tucking the thought away for the time being, I asked, "Any news?"

Frankie shook her head as her eyes traveled to Maia still holding on to me with all her might. "They told us to wait until someone come finds us." Her gaze, filled with concern, met mine. "Is she okay?" Frankie mouthed and I swear, my heart melted a little.

It was my turn to shake my head because I knew Maia wasn't okay. The last time she'd been in an emergency room had changed her life forever.

Nibbling on her lip, Frankie took a small step forward. "I'm…uhh…gonna go to the cafeteria, can I get you anything?"

The only thing I wanted was for her to stay. I couldn't tell her that but I could make it so she'd come back. Call it selfish, call it whatever the hell you wanted, but I needed her to come back.

"A coffee and maybe an apple juice for Maia would be great."

The smallest of smiles ghosted her lips before she said, "Okay. Be right back."

Unable and unwilling to look anywhere else, I watched her as she spun around and disappeared down one of the corridors. The direness of the situation well and truly sunk in then when I realized this was the first time since I got back that it didn't look like Frankie wanted to gauge my eyes out.

Shit.

Dragging some much-needed air to my lungs, I swallowed down the panic clawing its way up my throat. I had to be strong. For Maia. Whose arms were wrapped tight around my middle, fingers curled even tighter into the fabric of my shirt.

"Hey." My hand smoothed up and down her back. "You okay?"

I wasn't sure if Maia tried to shake her head or press deeper into me, but I did hear her words loud and clear even if they were muffled. "I hate it here. Can we leave?"

Gripping her shoulders, I pushed her back slightly so I could drop to my haunches in front of her. "I know you do, and I promise as soon as we know what's going on with Nan, we'll leave."

Pulling a face, she lowered her eyes, "I'm sorry. I didn't mean for it to sound like I don't care about Nan."

"I know, Maia." I tapped her cheek with two fingers until she looked at me. "I *know*," I said again. "We won't stay a second longer than we need to, okay?"

Eyes filled with tears, she nodded furiously. I pushed to my feet and hugged her close again. On days like this I found it very hard to not be angry at the woman who gave birth to my daughter. Because from where I was standing it was only a selfish person who could do what she did without even caring about the consequences or lasting effects it would have.

I gave Maia one more tight hug before I moved us to the seating area. No sooner had we sat down when I spotted a middle-aged doctor strolling toward us.

"Are you the family of Hes Calloway?"

For a fraction of a second, I wondered how the hell the guy knew that but then quickly realized he must have recognized Maia. Pushing to my feet, I nodded. "Yes, I'm her grandson. How is she doing?"

"My name is Dr. Mark Atwood." He tucked his hands inside the pockets of his white coat. "Your grandmother suffered a broken hip from that nasty fall she took."

Shit. This was the last thing I needed to hear. I knew the statistics when it came to broken hips and the elderly. A ball of anxiety formed inside my stomach, knotting and twisting until I felt bile coat the inside of my throat.

"She'll need to undergo surgery," Dr. Atwood went on. "We'll keep her here until she is strong enough for the surgery then she'll need help when she goes home. But that's—"

He trailed off when Frankie joined us, his gaze lingering on her for far longer than I liked. My blood burned with an uncontrollable need to wrap an arm around her and stake my claim. To tell this guy to keep his damn beady eyes to himself.

Because Frankie was mine.

To be fair, I never said my thoughts or feelings were anywhere close to rational. And I knew I sounded like an uncivilized neanderthal. But when it came to Frankie, nothing made sense.

I cleared my throat extra loud. "You were saying."

Dr. Atwood gave me his attention which I returned with my best fuck-you glare. Before he could speak, Frankie sidled in close. So close, vanilla and coffee teased my senses. Even more so when she leaned closer still and whispered, "Do you want me to take Maia outside?"

Behind my ribs, my heart did funny things I couldn't quite decipher. Emotion flooded through me, filling me with warmth. Our gazes met and held, drowning out everything else around us.

It was just me and her and I sure as shit hoped she could see the gratitude I felt. That she understood how much that one simple question meant to me. With a jerky nod, all I could get out was a raspy, "Please."

Without waiting another second, Frankie handed me the coffee she'd been holding and walked over to where Maia was sitting. She smiled then; big and beautiful. And I would have done anything in that moment for her to aim it at me.

But since my daughter was the lucky recipient, I couldn't bring myself to feel too jealous.

"Come on," I heard her say. "Do me another favor and keep me company outside? I don't like the smell of hospitals. It clashes with my perfume."

I chanced a glance at Maia who to my surprise had a small grin playing on her lips. Well, I'll be damned. Not even a second later, her brown eyes shot to me in question. Her shoulders visibly sagging with relief when I okayed her question with a small dip of my chin.

It didn't take her long to get to her feet. The moment she did, Frankie handed her the apple juice and then they started moving toward the exit. Unable to help myself, I kept my gaze firmly on them until they disappeared through the door.

When I gave Dr. Atwood my attention again, he looked somewhat annoyed. The guy must have been yapping away while my focus had been on Frankie and Maia. Lifting my shoulder, I simply said, "Sorry, what was that?"

He let a small sigh slip before launching into details of the surgery; everything leading up to it as well as what to expect after. Honestly, the more words that came tumbling out of his mouth, the tighter the knots in my stomach twisted.

The road to recovery wasn't going to be an easy one for Nan. Not by long shot. And even though she was in great condition, her age or more specifically the brittleness of her bones all counted against her.

"When can I see her?" I finally asked.

"She's resting now. The pain meds knocked her out pretty fast, but I suppose you can still go in."

13

GAGE

"I'm sorry I made you wait so long," I said as I came to a stop next to the wooden bench. Shoving my hands into the pockets of my jeans, I tried to pick up my jaw off the floor as I took in the scene before me.

Huddled together like two best friends, Maia and Frankie were paging through Maia's sketchbook. The one she had never shown anyone but me. That crazy warm fluttering I'd been getting a lot of lately made itself known behind breastbone once again. Burning so damn hot, I had no other choice than to brush my fingers over the spot.

Of course, Frankie chose that moment to look up. Her beautiful blue eyes widening as if she was seeing me for the first time. And if that hadn't been enough to kickstart my heart, the way her lips curled into a crooked smile sure as shit would have.

"Hi."

My lips twitched. "Hi."

Something else felt like twitching when her dark lashes lowered along with her eyes to study my mouth for a few hot seconds. When our gazes finally met again, hers was so unguarded it stole my breath.

And for the first time in a hell of a long time, I saw that eighteen-old girl who not only knocked me on my ass with her confidence but also managed to steal my heart right out of my chest with a single touch.

Movement in my peripheral vision pulled me from my thoughts in time for me to make out Maia's head first swiveling in my direction then Frankie's before something between a snort and a giggle filled the air shortly followed by an amused sounding, "Hi Dad."

Frankie blinked furiously, effectively breaking the electric connection between us. "Did you see grandma? Is she all right?"

I nodded but couldn't speak immediately. I was still somewhat taken aback by the version of Nan I'd seen inside the hospital. Eyes closed, skin pale, the woman lying on that bed hadn't resembled my exuberant nan one bit.

I didn't like it. I didn't want to be faced with Nan's mortality, not when she clearly still had so much life to live and love—and shit—to give.

This was all wrong. Nan was supposed to be home; cooking dinner with one of her telenovelas playing on full blast. Panic surged up inside me, its sharp claws sinking into my skin. I—we—couldn't lose her.

My heart somersaulted and right before it could break through its confines, warmth seeped through my pores and steadied its wild gallop. I blinked before focusing on the origin of the feeling.

Beautiful, long fingers were splayed on my arm in the barest of touches. A touch that I'd felt all the way to the bottom of my soul. Sucking in a calming breath, I let my gaze drift over her fingers, up along her arm before finally locking gazes with Frankie.

Once again, my heart picked up speed. Only this time it wasn't panic but something else entirely. She was looking at me; those blue eyes filled with concern and something else I couldn't put a finger on.

Could be that she—

"Are you okay?" Frankie's soft voice interrupted, replacing one thought with an entirely different one. A question that I couldn't answer honestly. Because no, I wasn't okay. I was far from being okay. For so many damn reasons.

But I couldn't say that.

"Yeah, all good." I forced the words past the scratchiness inside my throat.

A strange feeling zipped over my skin when Frankie turned those blue eyes on me again, studying me long and hard almost like she knew I was lying through my damn teeth and was deciding whether to call me out on it.

She opened her mouth; the tip of her tongue sliding over her lip, leaving a glistening trail as it went. One I wanted to follow with my own tongue just so I could have a little taste of her.

Then I spotted the troubled look burning behind her irises and my chest squeezed tight. I wanted a lot from Frankie but not her pity. Never that.

"What did the doctor say?" Maia's voice floated through the air. I wanted to thank every deity I could think of that she spoke before Frankie had a chance to until the uncertainty in my daughter's voice slammed into me.

It was starting to feel like my damn heart was being mistaken for a punching bag. And I was man enough to admit all these sudden emotions were throwing me for a loop. Because I had no answers.

None at all.

But I sure as shit was going to do my damndest to give Maia some sense of calm back. Even if it meant I had to leave out some of the scarier issues we might have to face. Stepping closer, I crouched in front of the bench and placed a hand on Maia's knee. "Nan has to stay here for a while." I tried to relay the information I got from the doctor as best I could, purposefully leaving out the danger of a broken hip.

"Was Nan okay when you saw her?"

"She was sleeping, but the doctor said we can come visit her anytime."

Maia's nose wrinkled and I couldn't even imagine the war she had raging inside her. As much as she hated hospitals, I knew she loved Nan more. "We'll get through this," I tried to reassure her. "One day at a time, okay?"

I saw rather than heard her work down a swallow before her head slowly bobbed up and down. Giving her knee one more comforting squeeze, I pushed to my feet. Frankie was standing just to the side of me; arms crossed in front of her, teeth worrying her bottom lip like it used to when she was nervous.

"I…uh…should probably get going."

Somewhere deep inside my stomach a cold, sinking feeling registered. I knew what it was. I didn't want Frankie to leave. Because I knew I couldn't utter those words, I chose different ones instead. "I haven't said it before but thank you for everything you did today." I looked over my shoulder at Maia who was staring a hole into the book on her lap. My gaze found Frankie's again. "And for helping out with Maia."

"She's really great, Gage." Franke's features lit up and fuck me it was beautiful. *She* was beautiful. "Hanging out with her was the best part of my day."

I couldn't help it, I just had to look to see if Maia had heard Frankie's words. And shit I wasn't prepared at all. My damn heart could hardly handle seeing my daughter—who had felt so alone in this town just this morning—peek up at Frankie with sparkling eyes and a grin on her lips.

Yeah, I wasn't remotely prepared for the sudden rush of emotion slicing through me. Or for my phone to suddenly beep to life inside my pocket. I knew the hospital sometimes sent updates via text so instead of ignoring the thing like I normally would, I aimed an apologetic look at Frankie as I fished out the device.

The moment I swiped the screen to life, a muttered curse fell from my lips. Maia was on her feet and next to me barely a breath later. "What is it? Is it grandma?"

"No." Keeping my frown trained on the screen, I stared at the message. There was nothing bad there—just a quick note to inform everyone that Adam would oversee the cooking when our shift started—but still my stomach bottomed out.

There was no possible way I could keep volunteering. Maia had no one stay with and who knew when—if—Nan would be well enough to have a teenager underfoot again.

"Dad?"

I looked up from the screen, my eyes instantly colliding with Maia's concerned ones. "With everything going on today, I forgot about my shift at the station tonight."

"Oh," Maia said. "And now you can't go because I can't stay at grandma's anymore." Averting her gaze, she swiped her index finger over the skin below her nose. "Will you have to stop going to the station now?" The question came out all wobbly, her shoulders slumping.

She might have looked like a sulking child but I knew better. My way-too-young-for-this-shit daughter was already blaming herself for something neither of us had control over. Another lasting gift from the woman who gave birth to her.

“Hey,” I curled my fingers over her shoulder and squeezed. “It’s okay. You know I—
”

“Maia can stay with me.”

Both Maia and I slowly turned our heads to look at Frankie. Shoulders pulled to her ears; she was still nibbling on her bottom lip again. “I mean if she wants to.”

Before a single syllable could leave my mouth, Maia turned to me. Eyes big, she asked, “Can I, Dad?”

I sure as shit wasn’t lost to the fact that there was no hesitation on her part. Something that has almost never happened with Maia. She didn’t trust people. Hell, most days I wasn’t even sure if she liked them.

Yet here she was asking me to stay with a woman she’d known for half a day. There was also the possibility she was doing this because she didn’t want me to have to give up my dream.

A whirlwind of emotions roared to life inside of me. Twisting and whirling, moving and shaking. I felt dizzy. Like my body wasn’t built to withstand a storm of this magnitude. Like the sheer pressure of it might rip me in two.

This was all too much.

“I promise I’ll take good care of her.” Frankie’s words sounded soft but close. I blinked and blinked again to clear the fog clouding my brain. And when things finally shifted into focus, I found that Frankie had indeed moved closer.

So close that I could see the freckle under her right eye. I wanted to brush my thumb over it before pressing my lips to the spot. But now was not the time to be thinking things like that.

"You don't mind?" I forced the words past the cactus stuck in my throat.

Those blue eyes never left mine. "I don't."

Brows furrowing, I looked from Frankie to Maia then back to Frankie again. "Thank you. I owe you one."

Frankie's lips twitched like she was holding back a smile. "I reckon it's more than one, but who's counting?" She stared at me for a beat too long and I could have sworn there was heat simmering in her eyes. But that might have been wishful thinking because when she blinked and turned her attention to Maia, there was no trace of it.

"See you in a bit."

Then she turned and headed to where I presumed her car was parked. As Maia and I watched her leave—my gaze naturally stuck on her swaying hips—I couldn't help but feel the tiniest bit excited at how the day had turned out.

14

FRANKIE

What the hell was I thinking?

Hands perched on my hips, I stared at the state of my kitchen. It looked like a bomb had gone off in there. A colorful sugary bomb. A mess that would take me a hell of a long time to clean up.

Time I didn't have because I still needed to get the guest bedroom ready for Maia. Which brought me back to the question: What the hell was I thinking?

That poor kid was going to take one look at the state of my house, turn around and tell her dad I was not equipped to look after her. The really scary part? I didn't think she was wrong.

From the little things I picked up over the course of the day, I realized Maia wasn't like any normal kid her age. Sure, being guarded and afraid of hospitals was perfectly normal but it just looked different on her.

Even now, hours after we rushed through the hospital doors, I could still feel the crushing way in which she'd gripped my hand. Could still see the ice-cold fear in her eyes.

I'd wanted to wrap her up in the tightest hug but something warned me she wouldn't have liked that.

So I'd simply held her hand until she decided she'd had enough.

I couldn't help but admire her even as my heart broke a little. She showed the type of strength most people twice her age could only hope to have. And I had to wonder if Gage had a hand in that.

Ugh, Gage.

As much as I wanted to dislike him—since I wasn't hating him anymore—I couldn't. Not when he was so wonderful with Maia. I swear, every time he looked at her or spoke to her in that soft, understanding tone, I felt my ovaries explode.

And when he turned those deep green eyes on me… Oh, no, we wouldn't be going down that road right now. Not when I had so much to do and so little time to do it in. Pulling in a deep breath, I stepped into the disaster zone aka the kitchen, grabbing stray spoons and bowls as I went.

I barely had time to drop them in the sink when a sudden buzz against my butt cheek scared me half to death. Pressing one hand against my racing heart, I pulled my phone out of my back pocket with the other.

When I saw Maddie's name flash on the screen, I quickly swiped the green button and pressed the device against my ear. I didn't even have time to speak before Maddie's worried voice filtered through the line.

"Oh thank heavens. I was three seconds away from a panic attack."

"Seriously? When did you turn into me?" I tried to make light of the situation, quickly realizing it wasn't the best idea. Of course Maddie was worried. Mrs. Calloway had left her studio in the back of an ambulance while Maia and I rushed out of there like two speed demons.

"Sorry." I tried again. "It's been a day, and I was just being silly."

Maddie sighed; the sound soft as it reached my ear. "Yeah, I bet. How's Mrs. Calloway?"

Dropping my chin to my chest, I pinched the bridge of my nose while I explained to Maddie what Gage had said. Even though he'd left it out—for Maia's benefit, I was sure—I knew how series hip injuries could be.

I couldn't even fathom what he must've been—probably still was—feeling. As a kid, he'd spent most of his time at Mrs. Calloway's place since his parents both worked long hours. Until they died in a terrible bus accident and she took over.

She was the only family he had left. Besides Maia.

My heart constricted a little again, and I sent a silent prayer to every deity I could think of to keep Mrs. Calloway safe.

"That's terrible." Maddie's voice drew me back to our conversation. "But you know it's not bad news necessarily. Lucetta's mom recovered with no complications at all."

I heaved out a heavy breath. "I know. It's all so—" The dull sound of an incoming message halted the words on my tongue. I pulled my phone away from my ear to see who it was from.

Gage: Had to get your number from Caden since you never gave it to me.

I was still frowning at the first message when another one came through.

Gage: See you in 10

My gaze shot up from the screen, frantically bouncing over the surfaces of my still-a-mess kitchen. How in the name of all things holy was I supposed to clean this up and get the guest bedroom ready for Maia in ten freaking minutes?

"No, no, no, no."

"What's wrong?" Maddie asked the worry in her voice multiplied tenfold.

I started moving as fast as my feet could carry me, grabbing dirty bowls and measuring cups. "Shit, Gage and Maia are going to be here soon, and this place looks messier than a teenage boy's room."

"What?!" Maddie screeched. "Did you say Gage and Maia?"

"Yes. I'll explain later." She was still firing off a string of questions when I poked the red button and tossed the phone onto the nearest counter. A dick move, sure. Tomorrow, I'd beg for her forgiveness with brownies and cinnamon rolls but right now I needed to clean like my life depended on it.

Turned out, with the right motivation you could get a lot done in ten minutes. Well, in twelve minutes to be precise. And although it wasn't spotless by the time the annoying *ding dong* of the doorbell chimed through the house, it did look fifty times better than it had when I'd walked through the door earlier.

Grabbing a dishtowel from the hook, I wiped my hands and made my way to the front door. My steps faltering a little when a nervous tingle danced its way down my spine. A tingle that'd turned into a big ball of nerves in the pit of my stomach by the time I reached the door.

I flattened my palm against the spot before dragging in a deep breath and opening the door. That deep breath I'd sucked in came whooshing out again the moment I laid eyes on Gage.

He was dressed in station wear. A navy-blue tee with the station's emblem stretched over his left pec hugged his torso muscular like a second skin. There was nothing special about the navy pants but the way the material clung to his legs was poetry in motion.

It was damn miracle I kept my little sigh from escaping.

"We're early. Hope it's all right?" Gage started. "But I still have a few things to check over at the bakery. And I need to drop by the office before I can head to the station."

Gage was still talking when my gaze flicked to Maia standing to his right. Half of her was hidden behind Gage's big body, her eyes trained on her shoes while her teeth sliced into her lip.

Something inside me twisted and slid into an unfamiliar space. A foreign part of me that had this overwhelming need to make this girl feel loved and wanted. It was completely irrational because obviously she was cared for a great deal.

Clearly, all the excitement of the last couple of days was messing with my head.

Smiling brightly, my attention moved back to Gage and his annoyingly handsome face. Which was sans stubble. His cheeks looked so smooth, I wanted to drag my palm over it just feel to it against my skin.

Ugh, here I go again. Focus, Frankie.

"Of course it's okay." Stepping to the side, I pulled the door open wider. "Come on in."

Gage moved to the left and motioned for Maia to walk in front of him. Clutching her book against her with one arm, she hefted her backpack higher over her shoulder before gingerly entering my house.

"Well would ya look at that, we meet again," I said when she walked past me. "I'm beginning to think you might like me."

Her mouth lifted into a smile I only got to see from the side before a soft "Hi" fell from her lips.

I pointed toward the direction of my living room. "You can just put your stuff in there, this one-woman-show still needs to make the bed you'll be sleeping in."

Her head dipped in what had to be the smallest nod known to man before she trudged further inside. My eyes stayed on her, taking in the slight slump of her shoulders, her bent head and careful walk.

It looked like she was carrying the weight of the world with her. And in some ways she probably was. My brain couldn't even begin to imagine the things she'd witnessed or been through in her short life.

Blinking the thoughts away, I angled my head back to the open door and almost suffered a heart attack. While I'd been watching Maia, Gage had stealthily moved closer. So close that I could feel the warmth radiate off his body. Could smell his woodsy aftershave. I even had a clear view of the hairline thin scar just above the right side of his upper lip.

Memories of the times we spent together as friends crashed into me with the speed of light. The laughing. The teasing. And finally the longing. Young and dumb, I'd pined for this man for years until the night he'd finally branded me with his touch.

The night I not only gave him my body but my heart too.

I swallowed the bitter memory away.

Squaring my shoulders, I met Gage's stare. The intensity in those green eyes stealing my breath and sending delicious shivers through my body. "Would you like to come in?"

His utterly sinful mouth curved into a smile that did funny things to my heart and made his stupid dimple pop. "I would very much like to come…in." The raspy tone of his voice registered in that sweet spot between my thighs. "If only I didn't have to go."

Whatever was left of my sanity went poof when he leaned even closer. "You're doing me a huge favor, Baker. I'll have to think of some *creative way* to thank you."

"You wish." Even as I said the words, I knew it was in fact me that was wishing but I couldn't let him know how he affected me. He'd have a damn field day with it. And to be completely honest, this weird banter we always had going was one hell of a turn-on.

Crossing my arms in front of my chest—to hide the pesky little attention seekers inside my bra—I tried to keep my face void of any emotion as I glared at him. In answer, his gaze flicked to my chest before he cocked an eyebrow and chuckled.

"See you tomorrow morning." He licked lips and leaned even closer. "Be sure to wear something see-through and sexy."

"Ugh." I shoved his chest, trying my best not to revel in the feel of his hard muscles against my palms. "You're an ass. Go away now."

More chuckling as he walked backward out of my house. He was still wearing that stupidly sexy smirk when I gripped the door and slammed it shut. His chuckle turned into a full-on guffaw and it took all my strength not to yank open the door and…

Do what, Frankie? The only thing you want to do is climb that man like a tree.

Great, the annoying little bitch that lived inside my head was back. With a sharp shake of my head, I told her to shut the hell up as I spun on my heel and met up with Maia in my living room.

I found her sitting on the edge of one of my couches. Her sketchbook was perched on the tops of her thighs, her laced fingers resting on top of it. Head bent; she was studying a spot on my carpet.

"I might be wrong but as far as I know it's only superman who can burn a hole through things with an intense stare like that." Maia looked up, her brows pulling into a deep V above her golden eyes. "Unless you're secretly here from Krypton to save the human race"

Her lips twitched a few times and just when I thought I had to try harder, the most amazing thing happened. A big open-mouthed smile lit up her beautiful features. My heart just about melted on the spot.

"I actually hail from Asgard."

Shaking my head, I smiled right back at her. "You and I are going to get along just fine, kid."

"Not if you keep calling me kid," she muttered under her breath. I laughed and felt the tension I had no idea was there leave my body. Maybe the same happened for Maia because her posture relaxed, and her smile went all the way up to her eyes.

I walked over to the glass coffee table in the middle of the living room and grabbed the tv remote resting on the edge. Turning, I made my way to where Maia was sitting. "It's all yours," I said handing it to her. "I've got a tiny mess that needs cleaning up but after that I'll be back to annoy you with a million and one questions about those pretty drawings you showed me this afternoon."

"I can help." Big golden eyes blinked up at me. "With the mess, I mean."

I parked my hand on my jutted-out hip. "A kid who chooses work over watching TV." Chuckling, I shook my head. "Your dad sure is a lucky so and so." Warmth enveloped me when she lifted her chin with pride, the slightest blush stealing her cheeks.

Giving her an approving nod, I spun on my heels and motioned for her to follow. Maia was silent as she trailed behind me until we stepped into the kitchen and a surprised, "whoa," escaped her.

I understood where it came from. My house wasn't all that big and lavish. I had the basics. Functional steel gray couches with pops of yellow and lime green in the form of scatter pillows and abstract art against my walls. The open plan space made it possible to have my farm-style dining table and chairs in the same space.

Simple yet functional was what I always went for.

Except when it came to my kitchen.

Oh, it was still functional…if you could call a place that looked like a sleek industrial kitchen *just functional.*

Two islands sat in the middle of the floor. One with a marble top and the other with a light wood finish. I had my stove and two eye-level ovens against one wall and a commercial-sized stainless-steel fridge against the other.

Three pendants with globes hanging at different heights ran through the length of the kitchen, bathing it in a warm white hue. But it was the wall-to-wall window in front of the sink and counters that stole the show.

Or at least the picture behind it did. Green stretched and stretched and just when you thought you'd seen enough;

the light color of the beach broke through before it bled into the deep blue of the ocean.

Some people found their peace in a meditation room or a reading nook. This was where I always found mine.

"We so need a view like this at our place." Maia's voice was soft and wistful as she moved around me and almost floated toward the window. I swear, if the sink hadn't been in the way, she might've pressed her hands and nose against the glass.

Because that's the kind of pull the view beyond had.

I hopped onto one of the counters and curled my fingers around the edge as I leaned back. "You know, you could always go grab your sketchpad and put what you're seeing on paper." I wasn't entirely sure why but some part of me figured she needed to forget about the events that happened today and from the little bit she shared with me, I knew drawing had to be her place where she found her peace.

Maia's eyes flicked to mine for a brief moment before she stared at the view again. "But I want to help you clean up."

"Eh, I'm almost done." I swished my leg toward her, the tip of my sandal tapping her thigh. "Besides you're so tiny, I might trip over you or something. So really, it's my own safety I'm thinking of here."

She was already smiling by the time she looked at me. "Safety is important." Was what her mouth said but her eyes said something else entirely. Something more along the lines of thank you and that had me feeling all mushy inside.

A mushiness that had me smiling like an idiot when she rushed out of the kitchen only to return with her drawing supplies not even a minute later. My smile stayed plastered on my face as I cleaned up the rest of the mess while Maia focused on what she was creating.

It was still there when I came downstairs after setting up the guestroom an hour later and found Maia exactly where I'd left her. Moving as quietly as I could, I gathered all the ingredients I needed for two cups of hot chocolate.

Once the milk was slowly warming up on the stove, I whisked in unsweetened cocoa and sugar. Then I broke a chocolate bar into smaller pieces and set it aside on the counter. By the time I pulled two mugs from the cabinet, the cocoa mixture was warm enough to melt the chocolate pieces.

Wooden spoon in hand, I stirred steadily until no solid pieces of chocolate remained. Pulling the mugs closer, I filled them three-quarters of the way with hot chocolate then topped it with mini marshmallows and a generous amount of chocolate syrup.

"Break time," I sing-songed, placing one of the mugs in front of Maia. After grabbing my stash of brownies, I slipped onto the stool next to her and jerked my chin in the direction of her sketchpad. "Can I see?"

She hesitated for a fraction of a second before pushing the pad toward me with her index finger.

I had seen some of her drawings, so I knew this kid had talent in spades. Still, I was overcome with amazement when I cast my eyes on what she'd been working on. My fingers hovered above the paper, following every line and stroke of her pencil in the air. My eyes flicking between the view and what she'd captured.

"Wow." I couldn't keep the wonder out of my tone even if I tried. "You're very talented, Maia."

I wasn't sure why but she didn't look like was expecting me to say that. In fact, she looked a little embarrassed which was confirmed when I caught sight of her rosy cheeks before she tipped her head down and a curtain of hair hid her features from me.

Without thinking, I reached over and settled my hand over her folded ones resting in her lap. She didn't even flinch and for reasons unknown, I felt like I'd just won a prize. Like I'd done something good and right.

Even more so when she slowly lifted her head and graced me with a small smile. "Thank you." Maia's eyes dropped to her drawing. "Sometimes when I feel overwhelmed, it's easier to draw than to talk."

Her gaze immediately shot back to mine; brows tightly pulled together. The expression on her face one of confusion, almost like she couldn't believe what she'd just told me.

I squeezed her hands once before pulling away. "I know exactly what you mean. It's the same for me with baking. It clears my mind and if I'm really lucky it will put some things into perspective for me."

Her eyes lit up with understanding. "Yes." The smile she gave me then was so brilliant, I couldn't help but smile back in response. One that grew even wider when she pulled her hot chocolate closer and licked her lips.

I grabbed the stash of brownies from the middle of the counter then shifted in my seat, making myself comfortable. Opening the lid, I let the decedent smell of orange and chocolate fill the air around us.

Maia closed her eyes and took in a big whiff of the delicious aroma before she opened them and trained her expectant gaze on me. I held out the container toward her. "Brownie?"

Head furiously bobbing up and down, she pulled out a chocolatey treat and immediately took a big bite. I held my breath. It didn't matter how many years I'd been doing this or how many people had repeatedly told me how much they love my baking, witnessing someone sample one of my treats—

whether it be for the first time or millionth time—always filled me with nervous anticipation.

That split second between the moment the treat touched their tongue and the moment the taste registered was always the worst. Because you didn't know what would happen. Their face could contort in disgust or light up with delight.

Maia's face did neither of those things. Her eyes fell shut, an elated "mmm" falling from her lips as she pulled her shoulders to her ears and devoured the rest of the brownie. When she'd swallowed the last bite, she slowly opened her eyes and stared at me like I'd just opened up an entirely new world to her.

"Wow. That was…" she tilted her head to the side slightly. "Yummy doesn't really cut it but I can't think of a better word."

I beamed. "I'll gladly take yummy." I jerked my chin in the direction of the container. "One more?"

Maia didn't even hesitate and by the time we'd finished our hot chocolates and she'd demolished three more ooey-gooey squares there was an easiness settling between us that I welcomed.

"Right," I said as I pushed to my feet. "Are we cooking from scratch or ordering in?"

Maia tucked a hand under her chin while drumming the fingers of the other on the surface of the counter. "Can we order pizza?"

I shook my head and walked over to the drawer where I kept my takeout menus. "Ew gross," I said pulling it open and retrieving the embarrassingly large stack. "Of course we can." Winking, I headed back to Maia and spread out the menus—which mostly featured pizza places—before her. "Take your pick."

Fifty minutes and two four seasons pizzas later we were both sitting flat on our butts in my living room with the Jonas Brothers blasting from my speakers. "They're not so bad," Maia said after song number six.

I grabbed my chest in horror. "Not so bad? Surely you can do better than that. I mean, just listen to those smooth voices." I tossed an old CD cover at her. "And just look at those pretty faces."

She eyed the cover and then raised an eyebrow in my direction. "Aren't you a bit old to be drooling over young boys?"

There was a moment, a fraction of a horrifying second, where I thought she was serious. Then her lips twitched, and her eyes sparkled with mirth. "You little sh…ampoo bottle."

Maia's lips slowly curved into a full-on teeth-showing grin that had my heart melting like chocolate in the sun. Gosh, I thought she was lucky Gage had found her but now I was starting to think that maybe Gage was the lucky one here.

She leaned back against the couch, resting her head against the seat. Her gaze landed on a spot on the wall, her voice soft and wistful when she spoke, "I don't remember a lot, but I do know my mom loved boy bands too."

My heart skipped the smallest beat. I'd wanted to ask her about where she came from but at the same time I hadn't wanted to seem nosy. But she brought up the subject so if I asked now it wouldn't sound nosy, would it?

Slowly scooting a little closer, I just about whispered. "Your mom…is she?"

Still staring at the wall, Maia shook her head. "She's not dead. She just didn't want me." Her brows pulled together. "But that was when she was…" her voice trailed off and grew even softer when she spoke again. "She promised she'd get clean and come back for me, but my dad and Mrs. Reiner doesn't want me to—"

Her gaze snapped to mine, the expression on her face telling me she hadn't meant to share as much as she had. "Can I uhm…" she pointed to the stairs. "It's been a long day. Would it be okay if I took a bath and went to bed?"

"Of course. Do you need me to show you where everything is?"

"I think I can manage."

I wanted to reach out to her. Hug her. Squeeze her hand. Anything to let her know she wasn't alone anymore, but I knew that wasn't what she needed. "My room is just down the hall from yours," I said instead. "If you need anything, just come find me."

Maia nodded then slowly pushed to her feet. I tilted my head back, carefully watching her and holding my breath as she stood there for a while. I thought or rather hoped she was going to say something, maybe give me an inch more but that never happened.

Rolling her lips inward, Maia pivoted and hurried up the stairs without giving me a second glance. While my butt remained rooted to the floor. I was still sitting there long after I heard her go to bed, trying my hardest to forget the way she sounded when she said her mom hadn't wanted her.

I couldn't even begin to imagine the pain that came with that knowledge. I'd never wanted for the love of my parents. I'd never felt alone as a child. And I definitely never felt unwanted.

My heart ached in places I had no idea existed. The things this poor girl must've gone through too big to even begin wrapping my brain around.

And what did Gage not want her to do? Surely, if her mom got clean and wanted to see Maia, he wouldn't stand in the way of that? Unless there was a reason she couldn't see her?

Dragging my hand over my braid, I dropped my chin to my chest and sighed heavily. This was one place I needed to keep my nose out of. It wasn't my business. With that thought, I pushed to my feet and made sure everything was locked and turned off before I made my way upstairs.

After a quick shower, I pulled on the first thing I could find. This one happened to be my favorite silky pink negligee. Dressed and hair combed out, I slipped beneath the covers and blew out a long, dramatic breath before falling back against the pillows. Next to the day of the fire, this one had probably been one of the longest ones. My gaze flicked to the book sitting on my nightstand. On a normal night I'd spend an hour or so with my nose buried in a book—true crime, of course. It helped me wind down and settle my brain.

Tonight though, my brain needed no calming. I was ready to dive headfirst into dreamland. That was until my phone buzzed on my nightstand. My first instinct was to ignore the thing but then I remembered Maia was with me and that Gage might want to check-in.

Groaning like an eighty-year-old going up a flight of stairs, I grudgingly pushed into a seated position and snatched my phone from its resting place. When I unlocked the screen, I found a few messages waiting for me. One was from Maddie. A photo of her eating a cinnamon roll with the description: *Sad day, it's my last one.*

I quickly sent a reply promising to bake another batch soon. I moved on to the second message and froze.

Brian: Can't wait to see you tomorrow night.

My eyes scanned over the message again and again while I waited—and hoped—for a fluttering of something. Excitement…anticipation… Anything really. But nothing came. Well, not exactly. A huge knot of anxiety twisted and turned low in my belly filling me with the urge to text Brian and cancel our dinner plans.

But I couldn't do that. Not when I needed him to get Gage out of my damn brain. Nodding once, I closed his message. I'd respond to him in the morning, hopefully, by then I'd be at least a little bit excited.

On to the last message and of course, just seeing his stupid name had the butterflies in my stomach performing some *Cirque du Soleil* act. I dropped my head back and glared at the ceiling.

"Fucking Gage," I muttered into the darkness as I pressed my palm against the spot where my butterflies were going bonkers. This was becoming rather ridiculous and a hell of a lot annoying.

Surely, the shithead shouldn't still be affecting me like this.

My movements were angry and jerky when I poked the screen harder than necessary to open the message. Then my heart freaking melted.

Gage: Is Maia okay? I texted but got no response.

Clutching the phone in my hand, I slipped out of bed and padded down the dimly lit hallway. When I reached the guest bedroom the door was slightly ajar. Still, I knocked softly. No response from inside. As careful as I could, I pushed open the door and peeked in.

Maia was curled up on her side, the blanket covering her rising and falling with her steady breathing. Smiling, I backed out of the room and made my way back to mine. I shut the door behind me and leaned against it to fire off a text to Gage.

Frankie: Just checked on her. She's safe and sleeping like a baby.

The dots started jumping immediately.

Gage: Thank you.

I moved to turn off my screen when another text popped up.

Gage: What are you wearing?

A half-hysterical laugh bubbled up when I looked down at my nighty and imagined Gage's face if I texted him a saucy picture. That hysterical laugh quickly turned into something else when my brain conjured up a million filthy things he'd text in response.

Just thinking about his gravelly voice whispering the dirtiest things in my ear had a shiver working down my spine and my lady bits tingling. Because I wanted that. I wanted him to say and do all the things that lived inside the darkest, dirtiest part of my mind.

I wanted it so badly which was why my fingers flew over the screen with my response.

Frankie: Don't you have work to do? Good night, Gage.

15

GAGE

"When a man smiles like that while looking at his phone it's usually one of two things."

I looked up from the text Frankie had sent in time to see Adam lower his big frame onto the couch opposite mine. He crossed his arms in front of his chest and my gaze flicked to the burn wound on his left arm. It stretched all the way to his neck. A visual reminder that no matter how fascinating the flames were, they were equally ruthless.

Without looking, I locked my phone and placed it screen down on the empty space beside me before I leaned back and met his stare. "Which are?"

"He's either looking at really hot porn or talking to the woman who stars in the movie inside his head."

Pretty fucking accurate.

But I'd be dammed if I gave the satisfaction of telling him he was right. I cocked my head to the side and smoothed my hand over my freshly shaved chin—a requirement for all firefighters. "And if I was talking to my daughter?"

Adam's dark brows pulled together. "Then I'd be worried about you, man. Because that grin on your face definitely wasn't the kind you reserve for family or even friends."

"Shows what you know. I was checking in on Maia."

Adam unfolded his arms and leaned forward. "So you were texting Maia or…"

"Frankie."

I wanted to punch the shit-eating grin off his damn face. Especially when he leaned back and spread his arms wide. "Ladies and gentlemen, I rest my case."

"Fuck off, Carlisle."

The asshole's lips spread even wider. "You know the more defensive you get, the more it proves my point, right?" When I just glared at him, he had the audacity to throw his head back and laugh like a damn hyena.

"I don't know what's so funny."

Adam wiped his hand over his mouth, his grin still firmly in place. "I'm curious, from the little I've heard it's blatantly obvious that both Maddie and Frankie would happily take a piss on your grave if you died today. Yet, here you are smiling like a lovesick fool over a text from Frankie."

I dragged my hand over the back of my neck and shifted my focus to where a couple of the guys were huddled around the pool table. It was normal to be curious, especially since he was engaged to Maddie who happened to be Frankie's best friend.

Hell, for all I knew he already knew the entire story and was just making small talk. Either way, I didn't want to sit and chat about my past with Frankie. It was our business and even if she told whoever would listen, I wasn't going to.

"It's a long story," I said when my gaze landed on Adam again. "One I am in no mood to talk about."

Both of his hands came up in surrender almost immediately. "I wasn't gonna push. I know better than most that there are things we just don't talk about." He dragged in a breath, his hand sweeping over the scarred skin on his neck. "Besides, I actually came over to ask you something."

"Yeah?"

He nodded. "The chief and I talked about it and with Wentworth moving away in a couple of months, there's a permanent spot opening up."

My heart jackhammered against my ribs. Once again the only word I could utter was, "Yeah."

"The position is yours if you want it." Adam held up a hand. "Don't answer yet, you have two weeks to decide. But both the chief and I feel you'll be a great asset to the house." He leaned forward again. Resting his elbows on his knees, he gave me a long hard look. "This position would come with a lot of sacrifices, the first one being your construction company. You need to decide what you're willing to give up for this job. This thing that seems more like a curse than a passion on most days."

Leaning forward, I swept my palms down my thighs before resting my elbows just above my knees. I pulled the inside of my cheek between my teeth to stop my immediate answer from spilling over my lips.

Because, shit yes, I wanted the permanent position. Wanted to answer the call of a roaring flame as desperately as I wanted to take my next breath. But Adam was right. This job came with sacrifices and the decision to make them wasn't just my own.

I gave Adam a sideways glance. "Two weeks, you say?"

"Yep."

"All right. Let me talk to Maia and Caden and I'll let you know."

With a firm nod, Adam pushed to his feet and headed to where the guys were laughing heartily over Simon's inability to sink a ball. I watched them, took in their interactions with one another and knew it was that sense of family as much as the need to run into a burning building that called to me.

As an only child, my circle had always been small but from as long as I could remember I'd longed to be part of something bigger. Because it didn't matter how much love I'd been showered with—and I'd been showered with plenty—you still found moments when you felt alone.

That changed when I'd met Caden and his family. They welcomed me with open arms and when my own parents died, Mr. and Mrs. Baker, along with my grandma, had shown up and stepped in.

Those years were some of the happiest of my life. Until I messed everything up and couldn't face anyone anymore. The loneliness came back tenfold. Until Maia walked into my life. Just as lonely as I was, and a whole lot more broken.

So yes, I wanted to be a part of this family but I needed to make sure Maia was one-hundred percent okay with it. It didn't matter how long or how much I wanted this, there was nothing in this world that could make me break my promise to Maia.

I could never make her feel unwanted.

And then there was Caden, who was as close to a brother as I was going to get.

We started our business with nothing more than a few degrees and a whole lot of determination. Together we'd built it into this amazing thing it was today. I didn't want to let him down by walking away from it all to chase a dream I'd thought was long dead and buried.

Scrubbing my hands over my face, I fell back against the couch. Suddenly my uncomplicated life seemed a hella lot complicated.

16

GAGE

Fingers curled around the steering wheel; I took in the house before me. It was early morning, too early for any sane person to be awake. But the moment my shift ended this was where I wanted to be.

I could easily fool myself into thinking that I wanted to make sure my daughter was all right. But that would be a lie. If she wasn't, Frankie would've called me by now. So no, I wasn't parked outside Frankie's house at ass-o-clock to check up on Maia.

I was here for Frankie.

Because shit, I needed to see her. I needed the banter, the look of both hate and want in her eyes. Needed to see her breath hitch at the sight of me. I craved it almost as desperately as an addict craved his next fix.

And it was that need that drove me out of my truck and up the porch steps to rap my knuckles against her door. A few minutes passed before the door finally swung open but when it did, all my blood rushed south with a damn vengeance. I swallowed hard; really, really hard, needing the sudden thickness in my throat and somewhere else to go down.

A damn near impossible task with Frankie standing before me looking like *that*. Her inky hair was a disheveled mess that looked more like sex hair rather than sleep hair. Those blue eyes were dark and hooded and don't even get me started on whatever the hell she had on.

A dark pink cotton gown of sorts haphazardly knotted around her middle with one of the sleeves sliding down her shoulder to reveal a lacy light pink strap. My fingers burned with the sudden urge to grab that knot and yank her toward me. To curl my fingers around the edges of her gown and rip it open so I could feast my eyes on what lay beneath.

I was pretty damn sure whatever it was would have me wanting to pin Frankie against the nearest wall and bury myself so deep inside her that I forgot my own name. Although to be fair, she could be wearing a burlap sack and I'd still want to do exactly that.

"What time is it?" Frankie asked as she swiped an index finger under her eyes. The sexy rasp of her morning voice not doing much to calm the illicit thoughts racing through my brain.

Shoving my hands inside my pockets—a piss poor attempt to hide my growing erection—I rocked back on my heels. "Early." I looked her up and down, desperately trying to remember that mankind had evolved, and it wasn't okay for me to throw her over my shoulder and disappear into the nearest cave where I could ravish her for hours. Days even. "Were you wearing that when you texted me last night?"

A deep frown that I wanted to rub off with my thumb formed on Frankie's forehead. It only deepened when she slowly looked down the length of her body. I followed her gaze, taking a long hard look at those incredible legs peeking out from under the hem of her mid-thigh length nightgown.

Inches and inches of silky skin that I wanted wrapped around my waist. Or possibly on either side of my head. Shit, this wasn't going to do a damn thing to get me out of my hard situation.

I flicked my eyes back up in time to see her pull the sleeve up and tighten the band around her middle. That would have been perfectly fine if she didn't straighten her back and tuck her arms under her breasts.

Not even the shoot-me-in-the-balls glare she was giving me could stop me from staring. I had visions of pressing them together, burying my face in the middle, and taking turns licking each tip.

The thought alone had me slicking my tongue over my bottom lip.

"Really Gage? Don't you think it's a bit early for you to look at me like I'm food?" It might've been my imagination, but Frankie sounded a little breathy. Maybe she was as affected by me as I clearly was by her?

Taking a big step forward, I peered down my nose at her. "Hey, it's been a long night and I'm *starving*."

I swear it felt like time stood completely still as I watched Frankie slowly tilt her head back. She blinked once, twice, her teeth sinking into her bottom lip. Before I could catch myself, I gripped her chin and used my thumb to pull her lip free. Gently tracing the plump flesh with the pad of my finger. It was cold and slick, and I wanted nothing more than to lower my head and sample a taste.

Frankie's breath caught audibly, my dick twitching in response. Her arms dropped to her sides, her mouth slowly opening. "Gage, I—"

I would never know what she was going to say because some dumb asshole chose that moment to jog past her house and yell out an obnoxiously loud greeting. That was all it took for whatever moment brewing between us to be lost.

Frankie took two deliberate steps backward and moved to the side. "Maia is still sleeping. You're welcome to come in, I'll get a coffee pot going while you wait."

She turned around but before she could take a step away from me, I curled my fingers around her wrist. I held on so tight I could feel her pulse hammer against my skin. "Don't walk away from me, Frankie."

A myriad of emotions flitted across her face. First confusion, then something that looked like sadness ending with indifference. That was the one that stung the most. Holding my stare, Frankie tugged her wrist out of my grasp.

"Weren't you the one who walked away first?"

I shoved my hands back inside my pockets and ground my teeth together. "Can we talk about that?"

"You apologized, and I accepted. So, there's no point rehashing the past, now is there?"

"But there is." My voice was harder than I intended. "Especially when you keep throwing it in my face and then refuse to let me explain."

"Explain?" Anger flashed in her eyes. "What's there to explain? You left me alone and naked in a tent then skipped town before I even woke up."

Frustration propelled me forward. Which meant Frankie naturally stepped back. We did that dance until she collided with the wall behind her. Giving her zero space to move, I loomed over her.

"You have to believe me, I never meant to—"

"To what? Make me feel used? Like I was nothing more than a cheap whore you could cast away after you got your fucking rocks off?"

"That's not—"

"Dad? I thought I heard your voice."

I looked over my shoulder and found Maia staring at us. Her confused gaze bouncing between Frankie and I. Dropping my chin to my chest, I muttered out a curse before taking a few steps backward.

"I'll be in the kitchen."

The words had barely left her mouth before Frankie turned and hurried away. I wanted to go after her, to tell her she had it all wrong. That I never meant for her to feel like that.

Instead of doing that, I walked over to Maia and hugged her. "Sleep okay?"

She nodded against my chest. "I did." She pushed away from me, her gaze briefly flicking in the direction Frankie rushed off in before settling on me again. "That looked tense."

This kid had always been way wiser than her years, it was completely stupid of me to think she wouldn't pick up on my and Frankie's past. Although to be fair, she did walk in at a rather interesting time and who knew how much of our conversation she heard.

Smoothing my hand through my hair and down the back of my neck, I exhaled. "Frankie and I…we might have some history. Unresolved history." Maia made noise, one that said it might be a bit more than that. "Why don't you go get your things, I need to talk to Frankie for a sec."

Maia pursed her lips like she was trying extremely hard to keep her words inside. On any other day I'd tell her to just spit it out already but for some unfathomable reason, I didn't want to hear what she had to say about this situation.

Especially not if she heard what Frankie had said before she walked in.

Figuring Maia and I had come to an understanding, I took two steps backward and pivoted. As I slowly made my way through Frankie's house, my gaze bounced over the furniture and walls, taking in the art and pictures a lot quicker than I would have liked.

But I knew I didn't have a lot of time to talk to Frankie before Maia would be down again and I needed her to hear what I had to say. Especially since my actions had left her feeling so horrible.

It wasn't long before I slinked into the kitchen. Frankie was standing in front of the sink, eyes focused on the spectacular view beyond the window. As gorgeous as it was though, it had nothing on Frankie.

Slowing my steps, I walked up to the island in the middle of the kitchen. "Frankie."

Her shoulders sagged, and she bowed her head. I couldn't see it, but somehow my mind conjured an image of her screwing her eyes shut and sucking in a deep breath. "It's too early in the damn morning for any of this, Gage."

"We're going to have to do it at some point."

Frankie spun around; arms folded in front of her, she glared at me. "Why?"

"Because," I moved around the island so I could stand in front of her. "I need to explain things to you." I ducked my head, meeting her icy blue stare head-on. "You were never just a means to an end, Frankie. My hand worked pretty fucking fine whenever I needed a release."

Her eyes bounced between mine, searching for who knew what. "Your mouth says one thing, but your actions said something else entirely. But you know what? It doesn't matter anymore. It's in the past. Water under the bridge or whatever the hell people say."

It happened so fast, I barely had time to register my movements before I felt the soft skin of her cheek against my palm. I brushed my thumb along her delicate cheekbone, my words whisper-soft.

"But it *does* matter." My face inched closer to hers. So close that I could feel the warmth of her breath flutter over my lips. "All this anger you're still feeling means there's something more here. You and I, we're not done. Not by a long shot."

My hand slipped into her hair, my arm banding around her waist and tugging her close. Frankie swallowed hard but not once did she tell me to back off. In fact when she tilted her head back those eyes of hers were dark with desire.

My mouth hovered over hers, our lips almost touching. "Tell me again it doesn't matter."

"I—"

Of course her damn doorbell would ring at that exact moment. "Oh for shit's sake." Reluctantly, I let go of Frankie and took a step back. My hand dropped to my crotch where I shamelessly adjusted myself. "We need to talk, but clearly that's not gonna happen right now. Have dinner with me tonight. I'll cook and once Maia goes to bed you and I can have this long-overdue conversation."

Biting her lip, Frankie's gaze slowly shifted from my groin to meet mine. "I…" she blinked a few times, her brows pulling together. "I can't. I have a date tonight."

A bucket of ice over the head wouldn't have had the same effect as her words just had. "With whom?" My voice was stern and demanding and I didn't give two shits. "Please tell me it's not with that dickhead. What's his name…Brick, Dick…"

"Brian," Frankie said through gritted teeth. "And who I choose to have dinner with is none of your damn business."

The doorbell rang again.

Frankie tried to push past me but my hand shot out, fingers curling around her wrist. "You're not going out with that asshole."

She stared at my hand holding her captive before lifting her gaze to mine. The biggest, meanest man would have nothing on the fuck-you glare she pinned me with. "One, take your damn hands off me. And two, I'll do whatever," she leaned closer, "and whomever I please."

All it took was one hard tug and I let her go, angst rushing through my veins at the sight of her hurrying out of the kitchen. I had half a mind to follow her and tell whoever was at the door that they needed to get lost.

I probably would have done exactly that if Maia hadn't chosen that moment to fill the doorway. "I'm guessing your talk didn't go as planned?" She hiked her backpack higher with one hand, her notebook safely tucked in the other.

I planted my hands on my hips and blew out an exasperated breath. "Seriously, quit being a smartass."

"I can't. This is you rubbing off on me." The expression on her face never changed, and I instantly felt tremendously sorry for whatever poor shmuck tried to mess with her. That one look was enough to make any boy run in the opposite direction.

Good thing I wasn't a boy.

"Yeah, yeah whatever, smartass." I walked to where she was standing and squeezed her shoulder. "You ready to go home?"

I was fully expecting her to be thrilled out of her mind to finally return to the space where she felt safest so when she chewed on her lip and aimlessly stared into the kitchen, I was a little more than surprised.

When her gaze met mine again, it was filled with uncertainty. "Wouldn't it be rude to just leave? I made the bed and cleaned up after myself in the bathroom but," she shrugged. "I dunno. It feels rude."

I should've known my daughter would be as taken with Frankie as I was. Not that I could blame her. Frankie Baker had that effect on most people. It was just a little staggering that Maia had taken to her so fast.

17

FRANKIE

In my fit of fury, I swung the door open and ground out "What?" before I even registered who was standing outside. As usual, this was all Gage's fault. How dare he walk into my house, put his hands on me, and tell who I can or can't see.

And how dare I like it.

I'd known for a while that my head probably wasn't screwed on straight, the current state of my underwear only confirmed that. Honestly, who in their damn right mind would be turned on by any of what happened this morning?

Me, apparently.

"I swear, I come in peace." My brother smirked, his index and middle finger forming a V next to his face. I wanted to smack him too. Just for the hell of it.

Instead, I stood to the side and motioned for him to come in.

He hooked a thumb over his shoulder when he walked past me. "That Gage's truck parked outside?"

I gritted my teeth. "It is."

"Oh." Caden waggled his brows, his features a little too cheery for my current mood. "Anything you want to tell me?" He made a show of looking deeper into the house before leaning in like he was about to tell me a saucy secret. "Is it safe to go in? I don't want to see his—"

"Maia spent the night with me, you idiot."

His brows climbed toward his hairline. "Someone's in a pissy mood." Without saying another word, he ventured further into the house leaving me with the urge to flip off his retreating back.

Rather than do exactly that, I closed the front door and leaned my forehead against it. All of this shit before coffee was too much. Way way too much. What I needed was a strong dose of caffeine and then some time alone with my little pink friend in the shower.

Maybe after that my brain would function properly.

Pushing off the door, I padded back to the kitchen. Gage and Caden's voices drifted through the air as they discussed some building project. Even though he kept talking, Gage's gaze found mine the instant I set foot inside the suddenly too-small space.

We're not done. I swear, I saw the words in his eyes as crystal clear as if he had just ground them out next to my ear. Naturally, that had my body suppressing some kind of shiver at the mere thought of his hot breath on my skin again.

Ugh! This was why I needed that shower a lot more than I needed my morning cuppa.

Squaring my shoulders, I tilted my head to the side and glared back a message of my own. *Screw you, Calloway.*

Unfortunately, it didn't have the desired effect. One corner of his mouth lifted and the look he gave me almost set my favorite pair of panties on fire.

When my brother finally noticed his idiot friend's attention was elsewhere, he twisted his big body to face me. Before he uttered a single word, I crossed my arms in front of me and asked, "Not that I am not happy to see my only brother, but what in the name of sweet treats are you doing here so damn early?"

My brother mimicked my stance, only he spread his legs a bit wider, and rocked back on his heels. "I have a great opportunity for you."

The satisfied look on his face had me mumbling "I'm afraid to ask," as I gingerly made my way to the coffee pot. I passed Maia on the way; she was sitting in the same spot as the day before, her sketchpad open, fingers flying over the page.

When I stole a peek over her shoulder, she turned her head and gave me a quick smile before returning her attention to her work. I wasn't even surprised when that one action made me feel all warm and fuzzy inside.

Behind me, the men picked up their conversation while I pulled three mugs from the cupboard. After filling them with the black tarry liquid that most likely flowed through my veins, I grabbed creamer and a juice from the fridge.

I set two of the mugs on the counter closest to the men followed by sugar and the creamer before placing the juice in front of Maia. I then retrieved my now-very-low running stash of brownies and put them next to the coffees just as I joined my brother and Gage.

"Talk to me about this opportunity."

Caden opened his mouth to speak but I couldn't hear the first few words that came out of his mouth. Gage slipped in beside me to prepare his coffee. That would have been perfectly fine if his arm wasn't brushing against mine or if his delicious scent wasn't so damn inviting.

Electricity skittered over my skin, my veins burning hot as my blood turned to molten lava. In an instant, visions of us flooded my brain. Visions of him lifting me onto the counter and spreading my legs with his big manly hands before he did wicked, wicked things to my body.

Oh for shit's sake, I needed to stop these kinds of thoughts in their tracks immediately.

Gripping the collar of my gown, I fanned myself while willing Caden's words to register in my ears.

"…and that was when he told me that they were looking for a bakery to provide them with treats for the employee lounge." He scratched a spot above his eyebrow. "I told him about you and guess what?" I shook my head, and he excitedly continued. "He'd already heard about Sugar Booger. He was going to approach you but then the fire happened."

"How is this an opportunity then?"

Next to me, Gage was finally done preparing his coffee but to my horror, he didn't move away. The idiot actually shifted closer if that was at all possible. Having him so up in my space was messing with my sanity and the hairs on my neck wasn't the only things standing on end.

Folding one arm over my chest, I slipped the hand of the other beneath my hair and forced my attention to stay on my brother rather than the man beside me.

"Well," Caden went on, completely oblivious to the tension mounting between me and Gage. "I told him you were baking for a select few clients from your home kitchen and he asked if you could bring him a sample box later this week." I wasn't prepared for the pride shining bright in my brother's eyes. Not even a little bit. "This guy is a big deal and if you're interested in corporate contracts, this will definitely be your foot in the door."

I was beginning to feel like a marshmallow with all the mushiness happening inside me. Stepping forward, I wrapped my arms around Caden and gave him the tightest hug. "Thank you." When I pulled back, I made sure to stand as far as away from Gage as I could without making it look weird. "Just tell me where I'm delivering the treats and I'm on it."

He pulled out his phone. "I'll text you the details because we both know you'll just forget it if I say it, or you'll lose it if I write it on a piece of paper."

He wasn't wrong.

While Caden's fingers flew over the screen, I made my way across the kitchen and slipped onto the stool next to Maia. Brows drawn together; she was still working away on her drawing.

When I'd first seen it the day before, it had looked like it was done. But somehow, she managed to add more life to it today with a few simple lines and shadows. "I didn't think this could look prettier than it had yesterday. Clearly, I was wrong," I told her honestly.

Her cheeks turned rosy and when she looked at me out of the corner of her eye, I had the urge to squeeze her against my chest. Man, I just wanted to hug everyone today. Everyone except Gage, of course. Him I wanted to smack…In the face…With my—

Stop it, Frankie!

Forcing my thoughts away from Gage, I set my elbow on the counter and rested my chin in my palm. "Have you been?" When my question was answered with a confused look, I clarified, "To the beach. Have you been there?"

Maia shook her head. "I've never been interested in going." The view stole her attention for a brief second before it was on me again. "Is it nice?"

"Well, that depends on who you ask. Some people think it's nice, others don't."

"And you?"

It was my turn to look out the window. "I like it." I shifted my gaze back to her. "We should go some time. There's this fantastic ice cream shop on the boardwalk that sells the best frozen treats you'll ever taste."

Her smile was back. "That sounds fun."

A sudden shiver danced down my spine and I knew Gage had moved closer. Sure enough, he appeared next to Maia barely a second later. Placing his hand on her shoulder, Gage bent forward. "We gotta get going. You still need to get ready for school."

"I'm packed we can go." Twisting in her seat, Maia looked at me then her sketch, and back to me again. In one fluid motion, she ripped the drawing from her book and slid it toward me.

My fingers gently traced over the edges, my mouth opening and closing a few times before I could actually speak. "You want me to have it?"

She nodded. "To say thank you for letting me stay last night." Biting her lip, she slid off her seat and gathered her supplies. Then knocked the breath right out of my lungs when she gave me a hug.

It wasn't long or super tight, but it had the exact same effect either of those would have had. And I instantly knew this little girl hadn't wasted any time crawling into my heart. Just like her dad.

"Until we meet again, Asgardian," I said with a too-wide smile.

Maia just shook her head and laughed before she turned to Gage and said, "I'll wait at the door."

He nodded in answer, his gaze following her for a few seconds as she trotted away. Then I was his sole focus. The intensity in those green eyes had my pulse doing a fiery dance. One that started low in my belly and settled between my thighs.

It was all I could do to not shift in my seat. Especially when his eyes lowered to my mouth, and he slicked his tongue over his lips. His gorgeous full lips that I wanted to both suck on and sink my teeth in.

As if he could read my thoughts, one corner of his mouth curved into a half-grin, the other disappearing beneath the sharp edges of *his* teeth. Then he stole my breath when he slowly leaned forward to growl next to my ear.

"Not. Done."

Before I even had time to tell him to piss the hell off, Gage straightened and marched out of my kitchen, clapping Caden on the back as he passed him.

"Ugh!" I all but yelled when the sound of the front door closing drifted through the house. "I freaking hate that man."

A gentle touch to my shoulder registered before my brother's words reached my ears. "No, you don't." Caden parked his butt on the stool Maia had vacated a few moments ago. "What happened?"

I shoved my hands through my hair before flicking the entire mass over my right shoulder. "He's an infuriating son of a—"

"I didn't ask what he was," Caden interrupted. "I want to know what happened."

Leveling him with a stare, I muttered, "He seems to think he can tell me who to go out on a date with."

His eyes went wide. "Wait. You're dating someone? How come I am only hearing about this now?"

"Maybe because my dating life isn't front-page news," I provided dryly. A heavy sigh blew over my lips as I pushed to my feet and started gathering the empty mugs. "Besides, I am not dating anyone. It's just dinner plans with a member of the opposite sex."

Caden grunted something under his breath. Turning from where I'd set the mugs in the sink, I faced him and asked, "What was that?"

He folded his hands together and rested his elbows on the surface in front of him. "You don't sound all that excited about your *dinner* plans."

That's because I'm not.

"It's early morning, you idiot. Who the hell is excited before the sun had time to properly rise?"

I gritted my teeth to keep the cuss words from spilling over my lips when his grin slowly spread wide. "There's something wrong with your face," I told him before I pivoted and busied myself with rinsing the mugs.

With any luck, the buffoon would get the message and leave. I needed some alone time to sort through this shitshow inside my brain. Alone time that was clearly going to have to wait since my brother decided to sidle in beside me.

Tapping his elbow against mine, he said, "Sometimes other people see things we can't or don't want to see. Like the chemistry brewing between two people. Everyone around them can see it sizzle and pop, usually waiting anxiously for that moment when the couple finally see it themselves."

Gosh, I hoped the tension between Gage and I wasn't that transparent. Still, I needed to know, "What are you on about?"

Caden placed his hand over mine to stop my furious scrubbing. I lifted my head and hoped like hell my feelings weren't etched on my face.

"Gage is a decent guy," he started. "Probably the only one I have never wanted to kick in the balls. He's crazy about you and as much as you want to deny it, the feeling is mutual. Why don't the two of you just stop dancing around what everyone else can see and finally give each other a chance."

I leaned forward and made a show of smelling his breath. "Did you add alcohol to your coffee?" Grabbing his wrist, I shoved the sleeve of his Henley up and inspected his arm. "Or maybe you're freaking high?"

With a sharp click of his tongue, he snatched back his arm and righted his shirt. "So much for trying to give my little sister advice."

"Unsolicited advice," I added.

I almost choked on a laugh when all my brother did was stare at me like I'd grown a third eye in the middle of my forehead. I was about to ask as much when he shook his head and muttered, "So fucking stubborn."

As it went with siblings, he smoothly switched to another topic. "I'm very happy with the progress the guys are making at the bakery. You'll be back in your kitchen before you know it."

"From your lips," I said as I grabbed the dish towel to dry my hands. "On another note, thank you for recommending me to that business guy. It means a lot."

He sliced a hand through the air, waving off my thanks. "I didn't do anything, James Meuser already had you in his sights long before he and I talked. And that was all you." His face twisted like he was thinking about something. "I don't think I've said this enough or maybe ever," he stepped closer, his big hands cupping my shoulders. "I'm proud of you. You started from scratch and built a reputable business without asking for help from a single person. That's so damn incredible. *You're* incredible."

A thick ball of emotion worked its way up my throat. I had to swallow a few times to get it to go down. Still, my voice was the slightest bit shaky when I spoke. "I'm telling Mom. I distinctly remember her warning you that you were not to make me cry."

There were a few seconds of silence before my brother's laughter rang through the air. "Come here, you little shit." In an instant, I was crushed to his chest, furiously fighting back tears.

"I better get going." We pulled apart and Caden started walking. I fell into step next to him. "What I said about Gage—"

"Don't, Caden." I shook my head. "I don't want to go into details but I've spent enough of my time on that man."

I didn't like the look my brother gave me just then but decided it was best to simply bite my tongue. You know, choose your battles and all that. Apparently, he had the same idea because we walked in silence until we reached the front door.

I quickly pulled it open and stood to the side.

"This is the last I'll say about any of it," Caden said once he was standing outside.

I closed my eyes. "Do you have to?"

"I don't know what happened all those years ago, but I know it was big for both of you. You might not know this but Gage changed just as much as you had. If he wasn't angry, he was sulking around. He rarely went out and never dated. And not just for a few weeks. For years, Frankie. Years."

My index and middle finger found the bridge of my nose and pinched hard. "Why are you telling me this?"

"Because your stubborn ass is going to make you miss out on something wonderful."

My jaw clenched in irritation. "If he's so damn *wonderful* why don't you go date him?" Beyond done with the conversation, I let out a terse "Bye," before shutting the door in his face and stomping up the stairs. Furious, I marched into the bathroom and tugged off my clothes before turning on the shower.

Not long after, a thick cloud of steam hung in the air, telling me my shower was ready. I stepped inside and immediately closed my eyes and tilted my head back to feel the warm spray of water on my face.

As the droplets rolled over my skin and down my body, I felt the tension of the morning leaving me bit by bit. That was until I imagined those droplets being replaced by Gage's hands and mouth.

I imagined him dragging his palms up my legs, digging his fingers into my hips as he lifted me and pressed me against the wall. I could almost feel his lips brush over my neck before he sank his teeth into the curve of my shoulder.

As the images in my mind started playing like some erotic movie, I smoothed my hand down my stomach. Lower and lower until I reached that spot that'd been throbbing and aching all damn morning.

My hand moved to its own rhythm as the movie behind my closed lids reached new heights. I'd been so wired, it didn't all that long to reach the edge and freefall into an abyss of ecstasy.

Slamming my hand against the tiles, I dropped my chin to my chest. Gage's name bouncing off the walls as I pulsed around my own fingers and I hated it. Hated that he had this hold on my heart. That even after everything this man wasn't even close to being out of my system.

In fact, I was starting to believe he might never be.

18

GAGE

Maia might've been quiet by nature, but I was certain she found it incredibly hard to bite her tongue on the drive back to our place. There'd been a few times where I'd heard her take a deep breath before I felt her questioning stare burn a hole into the side of my head.

She had questions, no doubt about that. I just wasn't sure how I was going to answer them. Because if she knew the truth, my daughter might never look at me the same way again.

That was something I would definitely not be able to handle.

Tension twisted and knotted in the pit of my stomach and I knew the sooner we addressed whatever was rolling around inside her brain, the better. That was why I turned to face her the moment my truck rolled to a stop in our driveway.

"All right, I can practically hear the gears inside your head turn. What's on your mind?"

Maia wrung her hands in her lap and bowed her head. Her thick dark strands falling over her face like a curtain. Or maybe a shield. My heart broke a little. For all the progress she'd made, she still felt the need to hide sometimes.

But then again, didn't we all?

Holding my breath, I gave her the space and time it took to collect her thoughts. Ten maybe fifteen agonizing seconds ticked by before she finally lifted her gaze to meet mine. What I saw in those golden eyes, almost knocked the breath out of me. And not in a good way.

"I don't know how to say it without making you mad." A deep frown pulled her brows together. "Not mad. Disappointed."

The knot inside my stomach tightened even more. My hand was over hers barely a second later. "Whatever it is, we'll work through it together. We're a team, remember?"

Maia pursed her lips and swallowed hard. "I want you to ask Mrs. Reiner for my mom's number because I really want to talk to her."

"I can't do that." The words were out before I could stop them. But in all honesty, my answer would have been the same even I had taken the time to think it through. I made a promise to protect Maia, no matter what.

And that woman was about as detrimental to my daughter as fire was to a dry field.

Unfortunately, Maia didn't see it that way. "It's not fair!" Yanking her hands out from under mine, she crossed her arms in front of her and huffed out a breath. "She's still my mom. I have a right to ask my questions and you and Mrs. Reiner are taking that away from me."

It was on the tip of my tongue to tell her that woman was as far from a mother as she could possibly be but by some miracle, I managed to keep the words inside. "Maia," I gently started. "You might not understand it yet but I—we're—doing this *for you.*"

"Whatever." She was out of the truck and into the house before my brain could properly process what'd happened. If it were any other situation, I might've had a stern talking to her about giving me attitude.

Today though, I just couldn't.

A heavy sigh pushed from my lungs as I fell back against the seat and pinched the bridge of my nose. That saying: *you have to be cruel to be kind* never made more sense until that very moment.

If only someone had mentioned that being cruel to be kind was the worst form of torture for both parties involved. Brushing my fingers over the left side of my chest, I rolled my head to the side and stared at the porch.

Mrs. Reiner's words ringing in my ears. *'There will come a time where you're going to hurt her to protect her. Are you sure you're up for that? Because believe me when I tell you, you'll be hurting just as much. If not more.'*

Yeah, she wasn't wrong. This pain, this marrow-deep pain hurt like nothing I'd ever experienced. But I'd take it every damn day if it meant keeping Maia safe.

***

"Why the hell aren't you at home sleeping?" Caden leaned back in his seat and tucked his hands behind his head. "You look like shit."

I flopped down onto the seat opposite his desk. "Working night shift is my excuse for looking like this. What's yours?"

"Haha." Middle finger aimed at me, he straightened. "Don't quit your day job, man. Your career as a comedian isn't going to take you very far." He pushed his half-full mug toward me. "You might need this more than me."

He wasn't wrong, I was in serious need of a strong cup of coffee. Leaning forward, I eyed the milky concoction, my face scrunching up with disgust. "I'd rather die before I drink that."

Caden laughed and took his coffee back as I pushed to my feet and poured a fresh cup for myself—no milk, no sugar.

"Seriously, why aren't you at home in your bed?" he wanted to know once I was back in my seat, sipping on my hot, tarry liquid.

Still holding onto the mug, I let it sit on the armrest. "I'm way too wired to sleep. First, there's the whole fire station thing and then Frankie hits me with this date bullshit. What the fuck is up with that?" Bringing the mug to my lips, I took a long swallow.

"We'll get to my sister in a bit but first tell me about the station." Brows pulled together, Caden rested his forearms on the desk. "Is there trouble?"

"Quite the opposite." I took another big gulp of my coffee, loving the way it warmed me as it slid down my throat. "I got offered a permanent position."

A low whistle filled the air and settled in the pit of my stomach. Volunteering two days a week had been one thing but doing it on a permanent basis meant I had to step away from our company.

A company Caden and I had built together through determination and a hell of a lot of work. Suddenly it felt extremely selfish to chase after this dream of mine.

"Did you accept?" he finally asked after a long moment of silence.

Eyeing him, I carefully studied his face for some indication of how he felt but his features remained unmoving. "Not yet. There's a lot to consider."

With a slow nod, he leaned back in his chair. "If you're worried about Blue Ladder, don't be. We'll figure something out. We always do."

"Thanks, man." I ran my fingers through my hair. "I still need to talk to Maia about it and of course there's Nan's surgery to consider too. If worst comes to worst…" I shook my head, unable to even think that far.

"Don't go there, man. Grandma Hes is too stubborn to let something like a broken hip keep her down."

Jerking my head in agreement, I pushed to my feet and crossed my arms in front of me. Now that I knew how he felt about the fire station, I could bring up Frankie and this bullshit date she was adamant about going on.

"What do you know about this asshole taking your sister out tonight?"

Caden blinked furiously at my barked-out question before shaking his head and chuckling. Tilting my head to the side, I glared at him. "What's so fucking funny?"

"You," he answered. "You and your twisted-up panties."

Spinning on my heel, I grumbled, "I'm all out of shits and giggles. See you later."

I'd made halfway to the door when Caden's "Wait" reached my ears. His voice was still filled with amusement. Fucking asshole. I stopped walking but didn't turn to face him. With my hand parked on my hips, I threw my head and stared at the ceiling.

Again, my idiot of a friend just chuckled. Muttering out a curse, I gritted my teeth and prepared to get the hell out of there when he finally spoke, "I don't know anything. Frankie only told me she was going out. But, if the guy is smart he'll take her somewhere nice away from Clearwater

Bay. And if he's not, they'll probably be at Olive and Vine—it's the only decent place in town."

I grunted my thanks before stalking back to my truck. Once inside I pulled out my phone and started searching for restaurants outside of Clearwater Bay. There was no way I was going to let Frankie go without a fight, even if that meant driving around all night or throwing her over my shoulder and dragging her fine ass home.

19

FRANKIE

"What about this one?"

Hands perched on my hips, I emerged from my closet to do a slow spin in front of the bed. Sitting crossed-legged on the edge, Maddie tilted her head and inspected my outfit.

The seventh one I'd tried on since she very dramatically informed me that my jeans and tee were not appropriate for a date. The newest member of the fashion police had marched me straight back to my room where she tortured me by making me try on almost every dress I own.

The one under her current scrutiny was a plain black dress that ended just above my knee. What made it special was the low V that dipped between my breasts and the delicate gold belt that miraculously made my waist look smaller than it was.

Already annoyed with this entire situation, I spread my arms wide. "And?"

Maddie's brows drew together, index finger tapping a furious rhythm against her chin. She sat like that for a couple of seconds before she jumped up and disappeared into my closet.

I took the opportunity to snatch my phone from my bedside table. Flopping onto the bed, I fell backward against my pillows and blew out a heavy breath. My eyes closed, and it didn't take long for Gage to enter my mind.

Not that he'd ever left.

Images of that morning in my kitchen had been running through my thoughts on a freaking loop. The way he'd pulled me close. His voice in my ear. The seriousness in his eyes when he told me we weren't done.

At the time, I'd assumed he was talking about our conversation. Now though, I wasn't so sure. And even more I had no clue how or what to feel about it all.

"What the heck?" Maddie screeched from the closet doorway.

I opened one eye. "What?"

"Get your butt up. You'll wrinkle your dress before Brian gets here."

I was pretty sure she was close to planting her hands on her hips and stomping her foot. Biting back my laugh at the mental image I was creating, I sat up. With my leg tucked under me, I very casually informed her, "Brian is not picking me up. I am meeting him at Olive and Vine."

"And this is supposed to be a date?" Maddie shook her head as she stalked toward me. Once I was in reaching distance, she gripped my right ankle to shove my foot into my glittery nude stiletto.

Her hand hovered above my left ankle, I smacked it away before she could manhandle it in the same way. "I can put on my own freaking shoes." I grabbed the other heel from her hand and slipped it onto my foot. "See?"

"You're very moody for someone who's about to go on a date."

"Maybe because I don't really want to go." The words were out before I could stop them. Covering my face with my hands, I fell back against the pillows again. "I should call and cancel."

The bed dipped. Maddie's fingers were curled around my wrists, prying my hands away barely a second later. "First, you're ruining your pretty makeup that you just spent over an hour on. And second, why do you not want to go."

As desperately as I wanted to tell her about Gage and everything that happened—not that there was a whole lot to tell—I knew how she felt about him. She'd probably drive me to Olive and Vine herself just to make sure I have dinner with Brian instead of Gage.

Even though dinner with Gage and Maia sounded so nice. *No, stop it. Gage is the enemy.* But was he really? Didn't he accuse me of not wanting to listen to what he had to say? And wasn't it me who was holding on to my anger like I was entitled to it?

Ugh, I'd never felt more confused in my life.

"This is about Gage, isn't it?" It shouldn't have surprised me that she knew. She was my best friend, after all. "What happened?"

I turned my head toward her. "He wants to talk….about what happened."

"And what do you want?"

My eyes went wide. "What, no '*he's a douche, stay away from him*'? Who are you?"

Maddie fell back against the pillows next to me and turned her face toward mine. "Some part of me will always be upset at how things went down but I realized if I had listened when I was warned against Adam, I would have never known what it's like to really love someone and have that love returned."

I opened my mouth to speak, but she stopped me. "I can't tell you what to do. No one can. You're the only one who knows what's in your heart."

"I think my heart is confused."

A sympathetic smile spread across her lips as she pushed onto her elbow. "And that's okay. Look, why don't go meet up with Brian tonight? It doesn't have to be anything more than two people sharing a meal. Maybe things will look less confusing tomorrow morning."

Holding on to that, I walked into Olive and Vine an hour later. I spotted Brian before he saw me. He was sitting at the bar; one hand on his beer glass and scrolling through his phone with the other.

For a split second I wanted to turn around and go back home but decided he deserved to hear from me in person that this would be our one and only meal together. Taking a deep breath, I lifted my chin and straightened my spine before I headed toward him.

I made it about halfway when someone grabbed my wrist and spun me around. "What the fuck do you think you're doing?"

My eyes locked with furious green ones. "I'm sorry? I think the better question is what the hell are *you* doing?" I gave his fingers around my arm a pointed stare before meeting his gaze again. "Let go."

Gage narrowed his eyes, the muscle in his jaw ticking at an alarming pace. Two maybe three seconds went by before he freed me from his grip. But then he stepped forward so we were standing toe to toe, chest to chest.

"You're seriously having dinner with that dickhead?"

I tipped my head back and glared. "What's it to you if I am?"

Brows pulled tight, he looked at something over my shoulder. "He so…" his attention came back to me, the intensity in his eyes nearly stealing my breath. "He doesn't fit with you."

My mouth opened but before a single word could roll off my tongue, Gage spoke again, "There's no way I'm letting you—"

"Let's get one thing straight. You," I poked him in the chest. "do not have a say in any of this. And I definitely don't need your permission for *anything*."

His eyes dropped to my index finger still hovering over his left pec, his jaw muscle jumping even faster than before. When his gaze met mine again, it wasn't anger I saw but rather determination.

Then the man robbed me of my sanity when he gripped my chin. He leaned in closer, so close our mouths were almost touching. My senses lit up, fireworks going off in my veins as I was assaulted with all things Gage at once.

What was left of my mind spun in circles. One moment I wanted him to let me go, the next I needed him to kiss me. To take me home and take care of the insistent ache between my thighs that he freaking put there.

"You feel it too," he murmured. "This thing between us isn't going away, Frankie." His eyes searched mine. "Why are you fighting it?"

"Gage, please. Not now."

His fingers slid from my chin up over my cheek before he buried them in my hair. His mouth was next to my ear a second later, his warm breath fluttering over my skin with every word he ground out.

"You keep saying that but sooner or later we're going to talk about everything. The past. The present. Everything."

Gage let me go and took a step back. "Enjoy your dinner." Spinning on his heel, he started for the exit.

He only made it about three steps before he turned back to me. "One more thing: if he touches you, I'll break every one of his fingers." Then he was gone leaving me to wonder why in the name of all things holy I found that very neanderthal statement so damn hot.

Shaking it off, I composed myself to make it to where Brian was sitting. By the way he was twisted in his seat, I was pretty sure he'd seen the entire exchange between me and Gage.

Great.

"Hi," I greeted, my voice filled with cheer. "I hope you haven't been waiting long."

He shook his head as he pushed to his feet. "Not at all." His gaze traveled up and down the length of me, appreciation burning bright in his eyes. This time I didn't wait for a fluttering or for electricity to roll over my skin.

There was only one man who had the ability to send my pulse skittering, and he'd just left the building.

Suddenly coming out to dinner didn't seem like the best idea after all. I sucked in a breath and smoothed a hand down my dress. "Brian—"

He stopped me with a small shake of his head. "I like you, Frankie. A lot." A rueful smile touched his lips as he reached into his pocket and pulled out his wallet. "But I think I might be too late."

Two bills were set on the bar next to his half-empty beer glass. "If things between you and that guy ever go south, you know where to find me." And then for the second time in less than five minutes, I watched a man walk away from me.

Feeling like I'd entered the Twilight Zone, I eyed the door for a few seconds before deciding to hell with it, I might as well stay and have a few drinks. Which was exactly what I did.

After three fruity cocktails, I had a nice buzz going. The kind where you're not drunk but relaxed and in need of someone to laugh with. Like your best friend. I fished my phone out of the nifty little hidden pocket of my dress and pulled up Maddie's number.

I was about to hit the call button when I realized she might be lying on the couch all snuggled up with her dog Sheldon and Adam. My heart squeezed almost like someone had wrapped a band around it and was pulling it tight.

In a blink, I went from happy and relaxed to feeling sad. And not because I couldn't spend a night out drinking with my best friend anymore but rather because I wanted to experience a little piece of what she had.

There'd only been two times in my life where I thought I'd get to live my happily ever after and both times I was left picking up the pieces of a broken heart. I studied the empty class in front of me, my thumb and index finger lazily sliding up and down the stem.

Maybe it was time to finally get answers to the questions I'd been so terrified to ask? Maybe it was finally time to get closure and move on?

My buzzed brain must've thought that was a really good idea because I was taking the steps to Gage's front door not too long after. Afraid I'd chicken out, I didn't even myself time to take a breath before I tapped my knuckles against the wood.

Movement from inside sounded almost immediately. My heart bounced around inside my chest so fast, so loud it verged on the edge of being painful. I had to resist the urge to press my palm against it.

When I thought it couldn't possibly get any worse, the door flew open to reveal the man who'd been haunting both my wildest fantasies and scariest nightmares. Hair still damp from a shower or a swim and wearing nothing but a pair of grey shorts, Gage stood with one hand propped on the door and the other on the doorframe.

Gone was my carefully planned speech. In its place, "I hate you."

"Do you now?" One eyebrow slowly arched as the corner of his mouth lifted into a smirk. "Where's what's-his-face?" He stepped forward, the smell of soap coasting through my airways and filling my lungs.

I wanted to close my eyes and just breathe him in but I would never give him the satisfaction of knowing how he affected me. Going on the defense, I straightened my spine and crossed my arms in front of me.

Looking him dead in the eye—and trying my hardest not to drown in the mossy green color—I drew strength from every horrible feeling I had ever had. "You couldn't just leave me alone? My life was fine, no, it was more than fine. But you just had to waltz back and turn everything on its head. With no regard as to how it will affect anyone.

"Because you just care about yourself. Screw everyone else, isn't that right? Ugh! I wish I could wish you away!" I was still talking when he started to close the distance between us. Naturally, I stepped back. "Wh-what are you doing? Gage, I swear, you better stop—"

Lighting fast, he snaked his arm around my waist. One tug was all it took for my body to be pressed up against his hard one. "Hey Frankie, shut up."

Then his mouth was on mine.

20

GAGE

The filthiest dream and sweetest promise all rolled into one. That's what Frankie tasted like. A heady cocktail, dangerously addictive. And I just knew nothing was going to be the same again.

But that was later's worry. Right now, I had every intention of kissing this woman so thoroughly that she didn't know whose damn air she was breathing. Turning my head slightly, I deepened our kiss. My tongue slipped past her lips, twisting and twirling around hers like a perfectly choreographed dance.

I buried my fingers in her hair while Frankie's hands smoothed over my bare shoulders, the heat of her touch searing me to my soul. She moaned. My dick twitched in response and I was helpless to stop my hips from rolling forward.

That earned me a little gasp that I swallowed down, too scared to break the kiss. The connection. The moment. Because it was everything. My hands traveled down her back and over the curve of her ass to grip her thighs.

Frankie must've sensed what I wanted to do because she jumped and wrapped her legs around my waist before I could lift her. With my mouth never leaving hers, I spun us around and pinned her against the wall next to the door.

My hands slipped under her dress, smoothing them up her bare legs until I could fill my palms with her ass. Squeezing hard, I pushed my hips forward at the same time. Another one of those moans I was becoming addicted to echoed from the back of her throat.

So needy.

So damn sexy.

I wanted to hear more of it.

Wanted to taste more of her.

Reluctantly breaking our kiss, I trailed my mouth along her jaw and down her neck. Taking my sweet time sucking and nipping on her skin while Frankie frantically writhed against me.

Abandoning her ass, I moved one hand to her breast. Teasing the still-covered tip with my fingers before circling and then kneading the plump flesh. Arching her back, Frankie pushed deeper into my touch.

Her breathing picked up and her hips found a new faster rhythm. So did mine. And I wanted nothing more than to push her over the edge. To make her scream my name. Unfortunately, or maybe that was fortunately, a little voice in the back of my head very rudely reminded me we were dry-humping on my porch…out in the open where anyone who cared to look could see.

Plus, there were things, important things, we needed to address.

Taking her face between my palms, I brushed my nose along hers. "We need to stop."

"No," Frankie whined.

"We gotta talk first."

Her eyes widened and those pretty, swollen lips parted on a huff. "Talk?" She looked down between us before pinning me with a stare. "Now?"

A chuckle rumbled through my chest earning me a deep frown and an even more pissed-off-glare. I kissed her then. It wasn't anything as deep or frantic as the first one. Just a soft, slow brush of my lips over hers.

But man, the way she immediately melted into me was some kind of high. And now that I've had another taste of this woman, this one far more potent than the first, there was no way I was letting her go…again.

I was going to tell her as much.

I pulled back just a touch. Far enough so I could look into her eyes but still close enough for me to feel her breath flutter over my lips.

"I don't think I need to tell you how much I want you right now. Hell, I've been fantasizing about having you like this for far longer than any normal person should." I paused, my gaze roaming over her beautiful face.

"So no, I don't want to talk—"

The words were barely out before her lips were on mine again, kissing me with a desperate hunger I not only understood but felt too. And fuck me, I wanted to give in to it so badly.

So, so badly.

But I couldn't. Not when the air hadn't been cleared. And definitely not before Frankie understood that I was playing for keeps this time.

Yet again, I tore my mouth from hers with great reluctance. "You didn't let me finish."

"No, *you* didn't let *me* finish."

Laughing, I dropped my forehead to hers. "What am I going to with you?"

"I can think of a few things." Hearing the smile in her voice, I immediately lifted my head to see it. It was as bright and beautiful as I thought it would be. But then again, everything about her was.

"Let me take you out, Frankie."

Her eyes searched mine, uncertainty lacing her words when she spoke, "On a date?"

"Yes. A date. We'll have dinner. We'll talk."

"There you go again with this talking business." She shook her head, her lips twitching like she was holding back a smile.

I brushed my knuckles over her cheek. "We have to."

"I know." Loosening her legs from around my waist, she lowered her feet to the ground. Hands perched on my chest, head tilted back, our gazes met. "I actually came here tonight to talk but then you assaulted me with your mouth and turned my brain to mush."

"You didn't seem to mind."

Her eyes lit up and that smile she'd been keeping hostage finally broke free. "When exactly will we be going on this date?"

"Tomorrow night. I'll pick you up at seven." I took her hand in mine, flipped it over so I could brush my thumb over her palm. "Say yes."

Frankie studied me for a long moment before she closed her eyes and drew in a deep breath. When her gaze found mine again, I didn't like the uncertainty I found there. "Don't make me regret this."

The words fell from her lips soft and hesitant. I understood why. When it came to romance, our history wasn't the best. Which was exactly why I was so determined to show her I'd learned from my mistakes.

Still holding onto her hand, I lifted her wrist to my mouth, placing a tender kiss against her thumping pulse. Smoothing my free hand over the curve of her shoulder, I hooked my fingers around her neck and pulled her face to mine. "One chance, Frankie, that's all I need."

"You really think—"

My lips were over hers, swallowing whatever doubts she wanted to voice. Only now that I was kissing her again, I sure as shit didn't want to stop. Not when she was kissing me back so fervently and definitely not when it felt so damn right.

That had my mind reeling with thoughts about how good, how perfect it would feel to have her naked body under me, over me, moving to the same desperate rhythm as mine. To have her hands all over me and for mine to explore every single inch of her.

As if sensing where my thoughts had gone, Frankie's hand slid down my side, her fingers burrowing into the waistband of my shorts. Groaning, I gripped her wrist and pressed it against my chest.

"Yeah, yeah, I know." She huffed. "Talk first." Gently shoving me backward, she moved to the railing, putting herself out of reaching distance. Which was a damn good thing considering how badly I wanted to pull her back into my arms.

Her eyes stayed on me as she chewed on her lip and pulled her phone from her dress. "I'm just gonna," she pointed toward the illuminated screen, "Call a cab." I started moving toward her but stopped when she shook her head. "No no, you stay right there. I'm way too wired and if you put on the brakes one more time, I might commit murder."

Well shit, I really wished she hadn't said that because the only thing I could think about was the state of her underwear. Or more precisely how wet they were. Rolling my lip between my teeth, I cocked my head to the side.

I could reach her in three easy steps. Kneel down, lift her dress and—

"Stop it," Frankie's breathy voice interrupted. "You were the one who wanted to talk so you're not allowed to look at me like that right now."

"Like what?"

Her tongue slicked over her lip, my gaze zeroing in on the movement almost immediately. "Like you want to eat me."

I grinned. "Oh but I do."

"You know what?" Frankie checked her phone before scanning the eerily quiet street. "I can just walk. It's not that far."

I was shaking my head long before she was done speaking. "You're not walking. I'd drive you but Maia is asleep, and I don't want to wake her or leave her alone. So either you call that cab or come inside."

Slowly turning her head, she eyed my front door. Brows drawn together and nibbling on her lip, she studied it for a few seconds before turning those pretty blue eyes on me. "I still can't believe you're a dad now."

A chuckle pushed past my lips. "Neither can I."

We were staring at each other, the air around us thick and heavy, filled with unspoken promises of all the things we wanted to do to each other. Or maybe it was just my mind racing with those illicit thoughts?

"I…uh…should call…"

"You should."

It would have been so easy to walk up to her and taste those lips again. But I knew if I did that I wouldn't be able to stop. My resolve was wearing thin and there was no way I'd have the strength to pull back one more time.

That was why I stayed rooted to the spot while she made the call. In fact, I didn't move until the cab stopped in front of my house. Silence stretched between us as I walked her to the curb.

"I'll see you tomorrow," I told her once she'd slipped into the back seat.

Frankie let out a little laugh laced with disbelief. "I guess you will."

Everything inside of me longed to reach for her; to pull her out of that cab, drag her to my bedroom and never let her go. Especially when she looked at me like she was right then. Blue, blue eyes filled with worry and fear.

Maybe fear wasn't the right word. More like apprehension. Like she wasn't entirely sure whether she could trust me. As much as I hated it, I was okay with it too.

Trust was something you had to earn.

And I was going to do everything in my power to gain hers.

"Sweet dreams, Baker." I closed the door and tapped the roof of the car twice before stepping back. Shoving my hands inside my pockets, I watched the taillights disappear around the corner.

I stood there for another minute before finally making my way inside the house. As I did every night, I made sure the doors were locked, and the windows closed before dragging my ass to bed—after checking in on Maia, of course.

I wasn't too surprised when Frankie and that damn kiss was at the forefront of my mind when I slipped beneath cool sheets. My skin hummed deliciously as I in very vivid detail recalled the taste of her tongue as it swept along mine. The feel of her skin against my palms. And the needy little moans that echoed from the back of her throat.

Shit, it was enough to make me hard. Painfully so. Closing my eyes, I sucked in a breath and squeezed my hard-on over my pants. It would have been so easy to take care of it. With my level of wired, it wouldn't even take that long.

I just didn't want to because the next time I came it was going to be when I was buried deep inside Frankie. With that thought, I squeezed myself one last time before turning on my side and drifting off to sleep, dreams of Frankie short on my heels.

My mind was still very much occupied with all things Frankie when Maia trudged into the kitchen the following morning. After taking a generous gulp of my coffee, I set the mug on the counter and planted my hands on either side of it.

"Good morning."

Headed to the fridge, she mumbled something that kind of sounded like a greeting.

"You still mad at me?"

"No," was what came out of her mouth but her tone screamed *'yes'*.

Sighing, I pushed off the counter and met her at the fridge. "Maia," I put my hand on her shoulder and squeezed. "I know you don't see it now but I promise you every decision I make is always, *always*, with your best interest in mind."

"I know." There was zero conviction in her voice and I hated it. Hated that she could even entertain the idea that I was doing this to…to what?

To hurt her?

To be spiteful?

I didn't even know what the hell she was thinking. A feeling of helplessness washed over me and settled under my skin. Gnawing and scratching like sandpaper to my bones.

"I promise, one day you'll understand." I motioned toward the breakfast nook. "Can I talk to you about something else? Two somethings, actually."

Eyeing me warily, her head slowly and subtly bobbed up and down. A muttered, "you're being weird again," pushed past lips before she grabbed an apple juice from the fridge and made her way to one of the stools.

Grabbing my coffee, I took a seat opposite her and chugged almost half of the tarry liquid down my throat. Deciding it would be best to start with the (hopefully) good news, I asked, "What do you think about Frankie?"

"I like her." Warmth flooded my veins at her immediate answer. Maia needed to be comfortable with whomever I brought into our lives. "She's a bit weird like you but it's a good weird."

Laughing, I shook my head. "I keep telling you there's nothing wrong with being a little weird. But seriously, you'd be okay with me taking her out on a date?"

"You're going out?" Her eyes went wide. "When?"

"Tonight. I asked uncle Caden to stay with you until I get back." I reached for her hand. "If that's alright with you?"

Her forehead creased, deep frown lines marring her skin. "You're asking me?"

"Yes, because this affects you too." I waggled my finger between us. "You and I, we're a team. And it doesn't matter how much I might care about Frankie, if you're not okay with it then I'm not doing it."

In hindsight, I probably should have talked to Maia before I asked Frankie out. I just wasn't expecting it to happen so soon. And as much as it would hurt me—and it would fucking hurt—I meant every word I'd said to Maia.

Slowly torturing me with her silence, she toyed with the juice bottle in front her. And as much as this was killing me I sat quietly and waited for her to work through whatever was going on inside her head.

When she finally looked up, I sucked in a deep breath and held it. I wasn't a praying man but shit if I didn't beg any deity I could think of to let her words be ones I needed to hear.

"Can we order pizza? I don't like uncle Caden's cooking."

My shoulders sagged with relief, lips lifting into a grin so wide I couldn't hide it even if I tried. "Yes, you can order all the pizza you want."

"Maybe for your next date she can come over for dinner?"

This was way more than I could have asked for and as much as I didn't believe in fate and all that shit, I couldn't help but think that this was all how it was supposed to be.

"Yeah, we can totally invite her over for dinner."

Giving me a quick smile, Maia unscrewed the bottle and took a sip of her juice. When she was done, she wiped her mouth with the back of her hand. She looked so much older than her twelve years. And I knew it was because she'd never had the luxury of just being a kid.

Not for the first time I wondered if I was doing right by her. If keeping her biological mom away from her was what she needed. Some days, like today, I felt so out of my depths and I was scared shitless of adding onto this kid's hurt.

Because heaven knew she'd been through enough.

"What was the other thing?"

"Huh?"

Rolling her eyes, Maia shook her head. "You said you wanted to talk to me about two things, Dad."

"Oh! Right." I brought my mug to my mouth and drained what was left of my coffee. "So, they offered me a permanent position at the fire station." When she just looked at me like I'd grown a second head, I explained. "If I say yes, my hours will be different from what they are now. Longer shifts more days a week. Is that something you'd be okay with?"

Her gaze dropped to the countertop. She studied it long and hard before finally looking up at me again. "You always tell me to follow my dreams wherever they may lead me. What kind of daughter will I be if I don't tell you the same?"

I was up and around the nook before she had time to blink. Wrapping my arms around her, I held her tight against my chest. "I love you so much, Maia. Don't ever forget that." I pulled back and held her face. "And don't ever change because you're one hell of an amazing person."

Her lip wobbled, eyes glistening with unshed tears that stabbed at my insides. "I love you too, Dad."

21

FRANKIE

Shifting the container of treats to one hand, I poked the doorbell with the other. As it had during the past twelve hours, my mind drifted to Gage while I waited for the door to open.

Or more specifically, I replayed that kiss to the point where I was beginning to think that I might have a problem. To be fair, it was one hell of a freaking kiss.

The kind that made your toes curl and your belly flip with anticipation. The kind that made you forget every kiss before that one.

Well, almost every kiss.

I could never forget my first kiss, especially not when it had been Gage to give it to me either.

"Oh my goodness, earth to Frankie."

I blinked furiously at the sound of Maddie's annoyed voice, heat rushing to my cheeks when her form came into focus. Hands parked on her hips, foot-tapping, she did not look happy with me.

"Uh, what was that?"

Before she could unleash whatever beast was roaring inside her, the door opened and Mr. Hamilton filled the frame.

"Frankie. Maddie," he greeted with a smile. "What brings you by?"

Maddie's anger dissolved in an instant and she greeted Mr. Hamilton with her usual sweet tone. After asking her about the studio and her wedding plans, Mr. Hamilton turned his expectant gaze on me.

"Would you young ladies like to come in? I was just about to have a cup of tea."

Lifting the container, I smiled at him. "Tea and cupcakes sound fabulous."

As we stepped into Mr. Hamilton's house, Maddie gave me a look. One that warned me our conversation from earlier was far from over. Thinking about it, I probably should have told her about Gage and the kiss and the date the moment I saw her, but she caught me right as I was leaving the house to deliver the treats to Mr. Hamilton.

And because my brain was far too occupied on the drive over, I'd spaced out on her more than once.

In my defense, anyone who had been kissed so thoroughly would have been lost in dreamland too.

Realizing I was about to fall down the rabbit hole again, I quickly reigned in my thoughts and followed Maddie inside.

As we walked deeper into the house, I noticed the scattered boxes. Some were stacked up, some were open. My gaze moved from the boxes to the walls and shelves, taking everything in.

Coming to a halt, I turned around to face Mr. Hamilton who'd been trailing behind me. "You're moving?"

His cheeks changed color but before he spoke, a noise sounded from somewhere inside the house. I would have looked in that direction if I hadn't been so fascinated with the way Mr. Hamilton's face lit up when he spotted something over my shoulder.

"You should have warned me we have guests, Ernie," an unfamiliar voice chirped. "I'm covered in dust and heaven knows what else."

Still, I didn't turn. I couldn't. I was too mesmerized by whatever was happening to Mr. Hamilton's features as he took in this stranger I had yet to see. It was like this person had flipped a switch by simply walking into the room. And by doing so, he'd added color to a black and white painting.

Maddie's elbow or whatever bony part of her poked into my back a few times. She was clearly trying to get my attention and I would give it to her the moment I was able to recover from my stupor.

"I had no idea they'd be stopping by," Mr. Hamilton said, his voice softer and gentler than I'd ever heard. "But come let me introduce you."

I chanced a look at Maddie and she seemed as confused as I felt. Confusion that only intensified when a man sidled in beside Mr. Hamilton and slipped an arm around his waist. The newcomer looked around Mr. Hamilton's age and with his rich dark skin and even darker eyes he was the very definition of tall, dark and handsome.

"Frankie, Maddie, this is Roland."

Maddie and I greeted him with a handshake, his touch as warm as the smile on his lips. "So nice to meet you both." He turned to Mr. Hamilton. "Would this happen to be the Frankie whose baked goods you can't keep quiet about?" Before he got an answer, Roland sneaked a peek at the container in my hands.

His grin spread wider to reveal perfectly white teeth. "Ernie has told me all about your bakery. I was very excited to sample some of your sweet treats until I heard the fire got to you too."

As he spoke, Maddie's arm hooked through mine and I felt it for the hug it was meant to be. Because no matter how ticked off she might've been with me, she'd always offer her comfort when she thought I needed it.

And I'd do the same for her.

"It was a very unfortunate event. And even though a lot of business owners suffered, I'm just happy nobody got hurt."

Roland's arm was around Mr. Hamilton again. "When Ernie told me what happened, I didn't even think twice. Just hopped in the car and drove straight here to make sure he was alright."

"It's a six-hour drive," Mr. Hamilton said, his voice soft and wistful.

"Auw, that's so sweet," Maddie cooed. And I had to agree. It was so incredibly sweet, and I couldn't imagine having someone care about you so much that they would drop everything they were doing just to make sure you were alright.

The two men shared a look and my heart squeezed in response. Wasn't that what everyone wanted, even when they wouldn't admit it out loud to anyone else? To have someone look at you like you and only you were their entire existence.

The longer I stood there the more I realized as happy as I was for Mr. Hamilton—and I was plenty happy considering he'd been all on his own for as long I could remember—I was a little jealous too.

Roland was first to realize we were all awkwardly standing there between the kitchen and living room. He smiled at Mr. Hamilton before turning to Maddie and me. "Come on, I'll make tea."

We followed him into the kitchen where we enjoyed two cups of tea and the entire batch of cupcakes I brought over while the men entertained us with the story of how they met on a dating app.

Love at first swipe, Mr. Hamilton had said. And it had to be since he was packing up his entire life here in Clearwater Bay to be with Roland. They were going to run a small B&B about an hours' drive away from Roland's hometown.

The excitement rolling off them as they spoke about their future plans and finally being able to live a life together was so infectious that both Maddie and I found ourselves bouncing to my car when we finally left the two men with a promise to stop by again before they leave.

"Wow, I have to admit I was not expecting that," Maddie said as we drove back to my house.

I hummed. "It was a surprise, that's for sure."

"You know, you didn't tell me how your date went last night."

"Uhm about that." Warmth shot up my neck and settled in my cheeks so fast I had to check if the heat in the car wasn't turned all the way up. "Brian and I never had dinner. I kinda ended up at Gage's place. We kissed and now he's taking me out tonight." The words spilled from my lips so fast, I had to suck in a breath by the time I was done.

Next to me, Maddie was being quiet. A little too quiet. I chanced a look in her direction. Jaw slack, eyes narrowed, she was staring at me like I'd grown a second head. "What?" I squeaked out.

"And I'm only hearing about this now?" she sounded offended.

I turned into my driveway and cut the engine. Twisting in my seat to face her, I explained, "I'm sorry. I've been a little lost in la-la land since it happened. It's freaky and exciting. It was just a kiss, one heck of a kiss, and somehow it's like my world has completely flipped over."

The way her lips stretched into a wide grin caught me by surprise. I was still frowning at the look on her face when she reached over the center console to grip my arm. "I know exactly what you mean. It was like that when Adam kissed me the first time. Actually, it's been like that with every kiss since."

She paused like she was working out something in her head. When she spoke her again I got the feeling the words coming out of her mouth were different than the ones she wanted to speak. "I'm so happy for you. Do you know where he's taking you?"

Normally I would've pushed her to really tell me what was on her mind but I didn't want my bubble popped just yet. "Not a clue."

"That's exciting."

"And a little nerve-wracking too." I pressed my palm against my stomach. "Even though I let him punch my v-card ten years ago, this will be our first date ever. How funny is that?"

Maddie squeezed my arm. "Would it help settle your nerves if I stopped by later? We can drink wine and listen to the Jonas Brothers while I judge every dress you pull out of your closet."

Even though she'd been there the day before to the exact same thing, my lips lifted into a giant smile as I said, "I'd like that."

After we said our goodbyes, I hurried inside and headed straight for the kitchen. It was blissfully empty since

Misty had already taken the day's order to Morning Kick and I'd told her to take the rest of the day off.

First date nerves were very real, and I didn't think I could handle a lot of her cheerful babbling while my mind kept drifting to Gage and what this date could possibly mean.

But now that I was standing alone in my very empty, very quiet kitchen, I had to wonder if that had been the best idea. Because with no Misty to distract me, my freaking brain was all over the place.

Over the next few hours, as I tidied up, it bounced from that night on the beach to the scorching hot kiss on Gage's porch. From the kiss it went to everything I wanted him to do to me which he very well would be doing later…after our date.

With that thought, I came to an abrupt halt. Gripping the waistband of my jeans, I pulled them away from my body to check on my wax job.

Thank heavens that was still as smooth as a jar of skippy.

I let out a laugh. Clearly, I had gone and lost the damn plot. Or maybe this was all Gage's fault for kissing me stupid. Then again if I could get kissed like that every day, I wouldn't mind giving up a few brain cells.

Because holy hell that man could freaking kiss.

Unable to resist, I closed my eyes and relived the firm yet gentle press of his lips against mine. His hands on my skin. His thick, hard—

Ding dong.

My eyes flew open. Damn rude doorbell interrupting my daydreaming. Huffing out an annoyed breath, I headed to the front door. A smile immediately stealing my lips when I pulled it open to reveal a devastatingly sexy man standing on my porch.

"Hi."

Gage's lips twitched a few times before one corner of his mouth curled up and his dimple popped. "Hi."

Standing to the side, I motioned for him to come in. "What brings you by?"

"These." He said as he stepped inside holding up a card with paint swatches on it. "You need to choose a color."

"Oh." I closed the door and aimed my frown at him. "I didn't know the walls were done yet."

A way too damn sexy grin lifted his lips. "They're not. I was just looking for an excuse to see because tonight feels too far away." Tossing the card over his shoulder, he stalked toward me like a predator advancing on its prey.

The butterflies in my belly fluttered about furiously while my heart found a new faster rhythm. The closer he got, the more my skin—amongst other things—tingled. By the time he was right in front of me, every cell in my body felt like it had been coated in lava.

Planting his hands on either side of my head, he leaned in close. "All I can think about is you and your hot little mouth." His nose brushed along mine, his breath warm on my skin. "And how desperately I want another taste."

Then his mouth was on mine, pulling a happy little sigh from me as I all but melted into his kiss.

Because holy hell Gage Calloway kissed like he was put on this planet with the sole purpose to do so. Every brush of his lips, sweep of his tongue touched me in ways no one else's had before.

I dragged my fingers through his hair while his hands found their way under my shirt. His palms touched my skin, calloused and warm as he slowly skimmed them up my body. Curling his fingers around my ribcage, his thumbs scraped over my breasts in the barest of touches but it was enough to send my pulse skittering.

Tearing his mouth from mine, he kissed a hot path down my neck and finally, *finally* closed a hand over my breast and squeezed. "The way you smell, the way you feel, it drives me insane," he rasped.

Completely robbed of my senses, my head fell back against the door and a low moan pushed past my lips. A moan that got louder when he curled his fingers into the cup of my bra and pulled it down.

Moving fast, Gage gripped my shirt and lifted it. He stepped back slightly, those green eyes turning darker and darker while his gaze bore into my heaving chest. "So beautiful," he murmured before ducking his head and closing his mouth over the tip of my breast.

My fingers threaded through his hair, the tips digging into his scalp while he continued to knead and suck like I was the most delicious thing he'd ever tasted. My blood felt hot while goosebumps littered my body and that pesky ache between my thighs became harder to ignore.

"Gage, please."

His entire body went completely still for a few seconds before he ever so slowly lifted his head. Pressing his palm against my cheek, he swiped his thumb over my bottom lip, his gaze zeroing in on the action almost immediately.

"I fucking love hearing you beg." His eyes met mine. "What do you want."

I flicked my tongue out, the tip catching the pad of his thumb. "I want to come." Smiling sweetly, I added, "Please?"

With a growl, he stepped closer and pushed his thick thigh between my legs, pressing it right where the aching and throbbing was driving me insane. Leaning forward, his lips coasted along my jaw. "Then come."

Fingers digging into my hips, he helped me rub myself against his leg. Creating delicious friction with every slide backward and forward. It felt so damn good I didn't even care that I was dry-humping Gage's leg against my front door.

I couldn't not when I was so close to having an orgasm. So, so close. Rocking my hips faster, I chased after that sensation that started building low in my belly. I was right there, carefully teetering on the edge, one hundred percent ready to fall when that stupid, stupid doorbell rang again.

Gage froze, his big hands gripping my hips so tight, I had no other choice than to stop moving.

"Noooo," I cried. Wrapping my arms around his neck, I pulled him close and whispered, "If we're quiet, whoever is behind the door will go away."

His eyes bore into mine, lips lifting into a crooked smile. We stood there, unmoving and completely silent, desperately willing whoever was outside to leave. Unfortunately, a whole lot of willing never accomplished anything because this time when the doorbell rang, it was immediately followed by pounding against the door.

"Frankie! Open up, it's Maddie."

"Ah, shit," I whispered through gritted teeth. Giving Gage an apologetic look, I explained, "She's not going to leave, she's here to help me get ready for our date."

He nodded in understanding but instead of stepping away like I thought he would, he reached between us and slipped his hand between my legs. With a soft brush of his lips against the shell of my ear, he ground out, "Don't touch yourself before tonight because the next time you come it'll be by my hand."

Then he finally stepped back but not before taking my mouth in a quick rough kiss. I took a moment to right myself as best I could before flinging the door open. One look at my best friend's face and I knew without a single ounce of doubt that she knew what I'd been up to.

Pursing her lips, she aimed her narrowed gaze at the man behind me. "I'm only going to say this once because I love my friend and I promised her I'd be supportive but Gage, if you pull the same shit you did last time, I will hunt you down and cut your balls off before shoving them down your throat."

Pretty sure my eyes bugged out of my skull because never in all the years I'd been friends with this woman had I heard her talk like that to someone. I was still gawking at her when a strange noise rumbled through Gage's chest almost like he was suppressing a chuckle.

Maddie didn't miss it though, her eyes narrowed even further, and I immediately felt incredibly sorry for Gage's balls. Because judging by the look of murder on her face, he was two seconds away from tasting them.

Unless I calmed the situation.

I opened my mouth but before I could utter a single word, Gage tugged me to his side. "If I end up doing something so monumentally stupid again, you have my permission to do exactly that. Hell, I'll even hand you the knife."

There were a few seconds of silence before Gage's voice sounded again. "But since I am not planning on going anywhere anytime soon, I think my balls are perfectly safe." He leaned in and pressed a kiss to my cheek. "I'll see you tonight." Then he lowered his voice to a gravelly whisper just for me to hear. "Remember what I said. No touching."

He stepped to the side and after saying goodbye to me and Maddie, he headed out.

Gage wasn't even halfway down the steps when Maddie came stepped inside, her scrutinizing gaze roaming over my face. "Are you blushing? I don't think I've ever seen your cheeks turn this color before." She inched even closer. "What on earth did he say to you?"

"Nothing." The word came out high and pitchy.

"Nothing huh?" Cocking her head to the side, Maddie smiled sweetly. "Some nothing that must've been."

I swear my cheeks burned even hotter which was utterly ridiculous. As was the sudden need I felt to change the subject. Still, that was exactly what I did. "I need to talk to Adam about this new violent streak you have."

Maddie shrugged. "You call it violent; I call it being protective of my friend."

"I love you for caring."

Pursing her lips, she hedged, "Why do I sense a but coming?"

"No buts, I just needed to tell you that." Wrapping my arms around her shoulders, I pulled her in for a hug. When I drew back after a few moments and found her misty-eyed, I frowned. "You crying, Maddie-Cakes?"

A frustrated noise came from the back of her throat as she stepped back and swiped under her eyes. "Ugh, I don't know what it is with me lately. Last night a freaking commercial had me sobbing into Adam's shoulder."

Moving deeper into the house, I jokingly said, "Maybe you're pregnant."

I swear, I could've heard a pin drop in the silence that followed. Stopping dead in my tracks, I slowly turned my head to look at Maddie.

Brows pinched tightly together, she was staring at her hands like she was trying to work something out.

"Oh shit. When was your last period?"

Her eyes met mine. "Uhm… I can't remember."

I was standing in front of her with my hands on her shoulders barely a breath later. "You need to go to the pharmacy and get a test. Come on, I'll drive." My tone left no room for argument.

Less than thirty minutes later, I was pacing in front of my closed bathroom door.

If I was that nervous, I couldn't even imagine what Maddie must have been feeling. Pausing in front of the door, I gently tapped my knuckles against it. "Everything okay in there?"

"I'm coming out now." Her voice was even giving me no indication of what she was feeling.

I stepped back when the handle started to move. Holding my breath until Maddie stood in front of me.

Eyes big and round, she stared at me for a few long seconds before she whipped the stick out from behind her back. "I'm pregnant!" Gripping my forearm with one hand, she bounced up and down on the spot. "I'm freaking pregnant."

She was in her own little world and I couldn't blame her for it. Letting go of my arm, Maddie covered her mouth with her hand. "Oh my gosh, I can't wait to tell Adam!" Her squeal had nothing on the look of pure happiness on her face.

I wanted to steal a sliver of it, just to know what it would feel like to be that excited over something.

Still beaming, Maddie gave me a quick hug before running off. She didn't get very far before she skidded to stop and spun around. "Crap. I'm supposed to help you get ready for your date tonight."

I waved her off. "I am fairly positive I know how to dress myself. Besides, you have news that can't wait."

Her smile was big and bright when she set off again. So was mine when I walked into my closet a couple of minutes later.

I eyed the dress I'd chosen for my dinner date with Gage. Just thinking his name had the butterflies in my belly going bonkers.

My heart did something similar.

I realized I didn't have to wonder anymore; I already knew the kind of excitement my friend was feeling.

And it was scary as shit.

22

GAGE

"Dad's got a date tonight."

We were barely inside Nan's hospital room when Maia blurted out the words. By the way Nan's pale face lit up when she heard them, I couldn't be too upset.

"Did he finally grow a pair and ask Frankie before someone else snatched her up?" Nan's eyes had a slight sparkle to them as she kept her gaze on Maia who was putting one of her framed drawings on the little bedside table.

With a few grunts and muttered curses, Nan tried to twist her body to inspect the frame. When she couldn't manage, her shaky hand slowly lifted, and she asked Maia to show it to her.

"Oh child, this is absolutely gorgeous." Nan's voice was filled with the same pride I felt in my bones. "Such talent you have." She stared at the picture for a few moments longer before handing it back to Maia with the widest smile on her face. "Thank you."

Her eyes snapped to mine, mirth shining bright in her irises. "Now tell me all about this date. I hope to all things holy that you're not taking her to that excuse of a restaurant here in town."

With a chuckle, I lowered myself onto the edge of her bed. "Now what do you have against Olive and Vine? They've got good food, great drinks and a fantastic atmosphere."

"Please." Nan shook her head and conveyed her disgust with a sharp cluck of her tongue.

In my effort not to laugh, it probably looked like I was choking on air. "What do you take me for, Nan?" I finally managed. "I made reservations at a steakhouse about an hour's drive away."

Her entire face lit up with so much pride you'd have sworn I'd just told her I'd developed a cure for cancer. She tried to push into a seated position but the pain proved a bit much so I stood and leaned closer.

Nan slowly raised her hand and pressed her palm against my cheek. "You're a good man, Gage and you deserve a good woman."

Emotion burned its way up my throat and stung the back of my eyes. I quickly swallowed it down. "Love you, Nan."

Patting my cheek twice, Nan smiled sweetly. "Remember safe sex is better than abstinence unless you want to make Maia a big sister."

"Nan!" Clearly being chained to a hospital bed had done absolutely nothing to dull Nan's personality. "In case you forgot, my daughter is right there. Within earshot."

"Pfft." She waved me off. "Never too young to learn about being safe."

The discussion about my sex life tabled, we spent the rest of our visiting hour going over everything for Nan's surgery in three weeks. To her credit, she didn't seem nearly as stressed as I was about it.

Not that I showed my concerns, but they were there in the back of my head slowly eating at my nerves. And as much as I tried I couldn't shake that awful feeling of foreboding. But if ever there was a day not to be thinking bad thoughts it was this one.

After years of pining for this woman, I finally had a date with Frankie Baker.

***

Curling my fingers around the steering wheel, I dragged a few ragged breaths to my lungs. And then did it again to try and calm my racing heart. This sudden bout of nervous tension licking its way down my spine was as unwelcome as it was unnecessary.

This was Frankie for shit's sake. I'd known her almost all my life. Felt something damn close to love for her for half of it for sure. And maybe that right there was why sweat beaded my forehead and my palms felt clammy.

This wasn't just any date. Not for me, at least. This was me finally chasing after the woman that should have been mine years ago. The only one to ever take up residence in my heart—besides Maia, of course.

With another shot of air to my lungs, my gaze flicked to Frankie's house. She was in there waiting for me and I couldn't help but wonder if some part of her felt the way I did. Oh, there was something there, that much was evident in the sizzling tension between us.

It was just so much more for me and I wasn't entirely sure how I'd feel if it wasn't the same for her.

Sitting in my truck like a damn idiot certainly wasn't going to win me any points. So after a quick check in the rearview mirror, I hopped out and made my way to her front door. I smoothed my hand over the row of buttons of my black shirt before poking the doorbell.

The drawn-out *ding dong* registered behind my ribcage, sending my already frantic heart into overdrive. Instead of pressing my palm against that thumping spot like I desperately wanted to, I shoved my hands into my pockets and waited.

I had no idea how long I stood there before the door swung open because when it did my brain cells along with my breath got knocked the hell out. I wasn't even sure how I managed to utter, "Holy shit. You look beautiful."

There were words far better than the ones I'd used but my brain simply couldn't produce them. Not with Frankie standing there looking like some kind of angel and devil all rolled into one.

I took a step forward to fully take in the beauty before me and holy hell if it didn't have my blood running hot. The top half of her dark blue dress—that clung to her body like a second skin—was held in place by a thick band that wrapped around her neck while the bottom flared out from beneath a shiny red belt, the hem ending just above her knees.

"Turn around," I begged, my voice thick and hoarse.

Frankie's red lips curled up slightly before she did as I asked. Since her inky curls were thrown over one shoulder, there was nothing obscuring my view. Balling my hands into tight fists, I kept myself from reaching for her while my gaze greedily took in the lace covering her skin.

The delicate material started at her lower back and stretched all the way to her shoulders. I wanted to trace the intricate pattern with my finger before I tested it to see how easily it would rip.

Shit! I needed to press pause on those kinds of thoughts at least until Frankie and I have sat down and had some dinner. A lot easier said than done when every single cell in my body vibrated with need for this woman.

Especially when she turned her head and glanced at me over her shoulder. Slowly batting those thick dark lashes, she slicked her tongue over her lips. “All good?”

A chuckle worked its way up my throat. “Oh, it’s so much better than good.” I held out a hand to her. “Come on, we better leave while I still have the strength to.”

Facing me, she put her hand in mine and let me lead her to the truck. Once she was seated and strapped in, I leaned closer to press my lips against the skin below her ear. I couldn’t help but smile when a slight shiver worked its way through her. “I’m very glad we’re finally doing this.” The words rolled off my tongue low and deep.

Frankie closed her eyes briefly before angling her head toward me. Our mouths were so close I felt her breath flutter over my skin. I wanted to kiss her. But I knew if I leaned in and locked my lips onto hers, we wouldn’t stop until we were both naked and satisfied.

Which suddenly didn’t seem like such a bad idea at all.

“Me too.”

I would have to have been an idiot not to hear the vulnerability in her voice. She was scared, no scared was too strong of a word. Maybe cautious was the right one? This was new territory for us.

Even though I’d been her first—and although she didn’t know it, she mine—we hadn’t done this. Sure we’d had plenty of meals together but it'd never been just the two of us.

That night on the beach had been the first time we'd ever been alone together for more than ten minutes. Unfortunately whatever memories we'd made were tainted by my actions.

So yeah, I completely understood where she came from. I deserved for her to be cautious where I was concerned. I was just going to have to work extra hard to prove to her that I wasn't that stupid boy who couldn't deal with his feelings anymore.

23

GAGE

"You're being awfully quiet over there. Should I be worried?"

We'd arrived at Hungry Grill, a steakhouse about forty minutes from Clearwater bay, a little while ago and in all that time Frankie hadn't said more than a few words to me.

Her blue gaze connected with mine over the rim of her menu. She studied me for what felt like an eternity before she lowered the menu and set her hands in her lap. Those beautiful lips of hers opened and closed a few times before she finally put me out of my misery.

"Just nervous, I guess." With a sharp shake of her head, she laughed. "It's weird. I've never been nervous on a date before. I don't like it."

I slid around the booth to sidle in beside her. Angling my body to face her, I took her hand while stretching out my arm over the edge of the seat behind her.

Before I could say anything, our waitress appeared. After she introduced herself as Wendy, she took our drink orders—which shockingly didn't contain any alcohol—

before she disappeared again. The moment she was gone, my attention was back on Frankie.

"I'm nervous too. I sat in my truck for I don't even know how long trying to work up the nerve to come to your door."

"Why?"

I brushed my thumb over her wrist, feeling a flicker of her racing pulse. Pretty sure my heart was beating just as fast. "I'm afraid I'll make a mess of things."

"Only if you leave again."

"Frankie, I…" I started but stubbornly the words remained trapped in my throat. Taking a deep breath, I tried again. "That night scared the shit out of me." I closed my eyes for a brief moment before opening them again. I didn't know how to say the next part, so I just spat it out. "You were my first too."

"Wha…no…but you—"

"Let you believe what you wanted to believe." With a chuckle, I dragged my fingers through my hair. "I was a player by association. Because Caden had a new girl almost every month, people just assumed the same of me. And I let them. It was easier than admitting I was waiting for my best friend's little sister to make the first move."

"Hold on." Frankie rubbed at her temples with two fingers. "You're telling me you knew I had feelings for you?"

"I suspected, yes."

"And still you didn't want to make the first move even though you had feelings for me too?"

"I thought I was being a gentleman because you were always harping on Caden about how he was chasing after girls. Then one day you told him maybe he should consider that there are girls who like to do the chasing too. I figured you were one of them."

A look of understanding crossed over her face, but it was gone a second later. "That still doesn't explain why you disappeared on me."

Smoothing my palm over my chin, my gaze flicked to the ceiling. I knew exactly how damn ridiculous my words were going to sound. Thing was, I owed her the truth no matter how absurd it was.

"That night when we slept together I felt things I wasn't remotely prepared for. And because I was young and stupid, I had no idea how to deal with it, let alone tell you about it. The first time I'm buried balls deep and my damn heart felt like it wanted to explode. Like it knew it wasn't big enough for everything I was feeling.

When you fell asleep in my arms the only thing I could think was how I wanted that for the rest of my life. The thought freaked the fuck out and I ran."

Deep lines marred her forehead. "That makes no sense, Gage."

"I know," I breathed out. "I know. By the time I came to my senses I was too damn embarrassed and too afraid to see the hurt I'd caused. So I stayed away. Figured I'd go the out of sight out of mind route."

I brushed my hand over the back of my neck. "By the time I was ready to face what I'd done, Jonah died and my world was flipped upside down again. Shit, Frankie, I know how all this sounds. I fucking know. And as much as I want to change the way I handled things, I know if I did my life wouldn't look like the way it does right now."

Her beautiful features softened; my heart squeezed tight in response. "You wouldn't have Maia."

"No, I wouldn't." I pressed my palm against her cheek. "I don't have many regrets but hurting you and not admitting how I felt are two of my biggest ones."

Her gaze roamed over my face and I couldn't help but wonder what she saw when she looked at me like that. Were the depth of my feelings visible to her? Could she see I would do absolutely anything to keep her?

"The way you left…" Shaking her head, she drew in a breath. "…hurt me so much. I was embarrassed, and I felt used."

"I—"

She held up a hand. "Let me finish." I nodded, and she continued. "For the longest time it had felt like I'd lost my roadmap and not because my ego was bruised because you didn't stay and cuddle. It was because I believed you were different. I'd felt it in my bones and when you left like you did, I couldn't trust my instincts anymore."

Wendy popped up again, giving us both a friendly smile as she placed our sodas in front of us. "You folks ready to order?"

Eager to hear what else Frankie had to say, I asked, "Could you give us a couple of minutes, please?"

"Sure, no problem." Slipping her notepad into the front of her apron, she turned and headed toward another table.

Once she was gone, Frankie turned back to me and picked up right where she left off. "I've been thinking about this a lot lately and I don't think I would be the person I am today if it hadn't happened. Any of it really, even Rick."

The mere mention of that asshole's name had me grinding my teeth and balling my fists. Unaware of my anger rising toward her useless ex, she continued. "I think I understand now why I'd been so incredibly angry for so long. It was so much easier to hate you than it was to…to admit that I missed you."

Inside my chest, my heart bounced around like a damn rubber ball. Over the years I'd envisioned many versions of this conversation. Some where she walked away. Some where she smacked the shit out of me. Some where she laughed at me.

But not once did I imagine her saying her what she just did. And yeah, to a lot of people that wouldn't have been something. But knowing that she'd spent even a minute of her time missing me was everything.

I didn't care that we were in a packed restaurant. Leaning forward, I took her face between my palms and touched my mouth to hers in a soft kiss. "I promise you I'll never leave like that again. I'm here. I've grown up and I know how to deal."

"I hope so." Her hands came up to cover mine. "Because this time if I wake up naked and alone, I'll hunt you down and saw off your balls before feeding them to Maddie's dog."

Chuckling, I kissed the tip of her nose. "The only thing I got from that statement was that you and I are going to end up naked."

"Of course that's the part you choose to focus on." She rolled her eyes, but I didn't miss the way her eyes darkened. And shit if that didn't have me going from zero to sixty in a second flat.

Lowering my hand, I slipped it under her dress. Slowly, steadily sliding my palm up the inside of her thigh, carefully watching her reaction. I wasn't one for public displays of anything but the need to touch her was so strong, I couldn't ignore it.

And by the way her eyes darkened even more as she sank her teeth into her bottom lip, I didn't think she minded one bit. Especially not when she spread her legs a little too.

Up and up my hand moved until my fingers brushed over the front of her underwear.

"Alright, what are you hungry for tonight?" Wendy's voice sliced into our lust bubble. Luckily some part of my brain was still intact, and it reminded me not to make any sudden movements less I wanted to draw attention to where my hand was.

I gave Frankie's leg a gentle squeeze before discreetly pulling it out from under her dress. "What are you hungry for?" From the sound of my low-pitched voice, it was very evident which part of my brain was in control again.

Those sexy lips that I desperately wanted wrapped around certain parts of me rolled inward over her teeth. Gaze bouncing between my mouth and eyes Frankie said, "I want a *thick*, juicy steak."

Fuck me, this woman was going to be the sole cause of my demise.

"And how would you like it done?" Our waitress cheerily asked.

Frankie's mouth moved again, but I didn't hear a single thing she said. Not when my mind was flooded with images of me slipping under the table. Her fingers in my hair. My mouth—

"And for you, sir?"

I blinked and blinked again until Frankie's beautiful but amused face came into view. "What was that?"

The corner of her mouth lifted into a sinful smile. "The waitress wants your order."

It took me a moment but when her words finally sank in, I realized I'd been lost in freaking la-la land again. Shaking my head slightly, I swiped a hand over my mouth and turned my attention to Wendy.

"I'll have the same, thanks."

Her fingers flew over the notepad as she jotted down my order. Once she was done, she slipped the pad into her apron and promised to be back with our food soon. The moment she pivoted; my attention was back on Frankie again.

"What are you doing to me?"

Her blue gaze bore into mine, setting me on fire from the inside out. "Probably the same thing you're doing to me."

24

GAGE

We spent the rest of our dinner catching each other up on everything we'd been up to over the years. Frankie told me about how supportive her family had been when she chose to start Sugar Booger instead of furthering her education.

I told her how difficult it was to switch from firefighting to construction and how surprised I was when I enjoyed it almost just as much in the end.

We talked about anything and everything and in those moments it almost felt as if no time had passed at all. It was like we were back in her parents' living room, sitting crossed-legged on the floor just getting to know each other.

Of course, this was so much better because back then we'd always had someone there with us. Whether it was Caden and his string of girlfriends or Maddie, there'd always been someone.

Even now, we weren't fully alone. I planned to rectify that. Leaning closer, I eyed our empty dinner plates before turning my attention to her. Unable to resist touching her in some way, I scraped my thumb over her jaw.

"What do you say we skip dessert and get out of here?"

Frankie slicked her tongue over her lip and it took every ounce of willpower I possessed not to surge forward and suck it into my mouth. Especially now that I'd said everything I needed to say and there was nothing stopping me from having her.

Her mind must have been somewhere similar because her voice was so sexy and breathy when she spoke. "I like the sound of that."

Her words were barely out when my hand shot up to call our waitress and ask for the bill. That delicious tension that was always present between me and Frankie found new heights in the moments we waited to pay our bill and hurry back to my truck.

The sound of the doors slamming shut had barely registered before I twisted in my seat. Hooking my fingers around the back of Frankie's neck, I pulled her face to mine. "I've been waiting all fucking night to do this."

I sealed my mouth over hers; finally taking the damn kiss I'd been craving since I'd left her kitchen earlier in the day. And just like then she tasted like broken glass scraping over my skin. Like ruin and salvation, all rolled into one.

And like the damn addict I was, I couldn't get enough.

My hand moved from her neck up into her hair, burying my fingers in the silky strands. While Frankie's palms flattened against my pecs. My heart slammed against my ribs with a ferociousness I hardly recognized.

I closed my hand over hers and pressed it against that spot on my chest. Breaking our kiss to whisper against her lips, "You feel that? You do that to me, Frankie. Only you."

Those blue eyes I wanted to drown in widened to their max, her tongue slowly sliding over her bottom lip. Something that looked a hell of a lot like uncertainty crept over her face and settled behind her irises.

I'd said the wrong thing. Could see that it was too much too soon for her. So I saved the moment by taking her other hand and dragging it down my body until her palm skimmed over my erection.

Curving up one corner of my mouth, I said, "You do that to me too."

The worry or whatever the hell it was that I'd seen in her eyes moments ago instantly dissolved. In its place nothing but white-hot need. And I was perfectly fine with that. It didn't matter how long I'd have to wait to tell her the words that had been burning up my insides for years.

Because I'd wait. For her, I'd fucking wait.

Whatever was left of my sanity disappeared when Frankie interrupted my thoughts by tightening her hold on my dick. "I can help with this," she purred.

"Mmm," I groaned. "You certainly can but not yet. Not here." I inched closer, our mouths barely touching. "Because when we finally fuck, I want you flat on your back sprawled out beneath me so I can sample every delicious inch of you."

Frankie opened her mouth like she was about to protest. I scraped my thumb over her lips. "That doesn't mean I'm going to leave you wet and needy." Slipping my hand under her dress, my fingers coasted over the center of her underwear in the barest of touches.

So wet.

So ready.

Closing the distance, I kissed her again. Only this time it wasn't slow and sweet. I plundered her mouth, greedily tasting her like a ravenous beast.

"Get on my lap," I rasped between licking and sucking on her tongue.

Frankie didn't hesitate. Planting her hand on my shoulder, she slid across the seat and moved to straddle me. My fingers found her hips and held tight, keeping her on her knees hovering over my thighs.

"Wha—"

"Show me." I gripped the hem of her pretty little dress and pushed it up. "Show me what you do when you're alone in your bed at night."

One perfectly shaped brow slowly climbed up. "You want to see me touch myself? Like this?" Not giving two shits that we were sitting in a parking lot filled with cars and chattering people, she slid her hand up and cupped her breast.

"Lower."

With the most sinful grin playing on her lips, she dragged her hand down over her stomach before slipping it into her panties. Her hips flexed forward not even a second later, a pleasure-filled sigh short on its heels.

My gaze flicked to her hand steadily moving between her legs. "I bet you're fucking soaked."

"Yes." I wasn't sure if it was a word or a moan.

"Are you imagining it's my cock inside you right now?"

Her breath caught; head rolling back, eyes falling shut. "Mmm Hmm."

I gripped her chin again. "Eyes on me."

Her darkened blue gaze slammed into mine, stealing my breath. My blood instantly turning into molten lava. "Tell me how it feels."

"So good." Her words feathered over my skin like a live wire scraping over a wet surface. Its insistent zipping and zapping threatening to burn me right where I sat.

And, holy shit, I'd let it.

Frankie moaned again, this one louder and longer. Her hand moved faster, her breathing coming in short bursts. She was close, and I wanted nothing more than to reach inside my pants and stroke my cock in tandem with her movements but this wasn't about my pleasure.

So instead of taking care of the ache between my legs, I lowered my head and closed my mouth over her still-covered breast.

"Oh," Frankie whimpered right before her legs shook and a low, "Mmm," echoed from the back of her throat.

I dropped my head back, shamelessly studying the look of pure bliss cross over her features. It was damn beautiful and I couldn't wait to see it again.

Capturing her chin with one hand, I lowered the other to curl around the wrist nestled between her thighs. "You're beautiful when you come." Tugging gently, I pulled her hand out from between her legs and immediately wrapped my lips around the fingers that had just been inside her.

Her eyes went wide and judging by the wicked way they darkened, I didn't think it mattered that she'd just had an orgasm.

"And you taste delicious too," I said as I pulled them out. "Now let's go home so I can have my fill of you."

25

FRANKIE

this."

I'd barely turned to shut the door when Gage pounced. With his front against my back, I was pressed against the door while his lips coasted over my neck. Goosebumps littered my skin and when one hand smoothed over the curve of my hip and the other caressed my breast, I couldn't stop the shiver dancing down my spine.

My head tipped forward; a slow "mmm" echoing from the back of my throat as I arched my back to press deeper into his touch.

"Oh, Frankie," Gage murmured, his voice low and gravelly. "Do you have any idea how long I've wanted this?" Teeth scraped my skin while his hand traveled lower. "How many times I've fucked my hand imagining it was you?"

Lower and lower he went until his palm touched my inner thigh. Arching my back even more, I pushed my butt back against his erection. He groaned. The sound of it rumbling through his chest almost like a beast pacing its cage, just waiting to escape.

Gage's mouth hovered over my skin, his breath hot while he dragged his palm up the inside of my leg. Up and up he went, reaching the edge of my underwear in no time. It didn't matter that I'd had an orgasm less than an hour ago, I was all hot and bothered again.

Not that I'd cooled down in the slightest after the little episode in his truck earlier—which I still couldn't believe I'd done. I was as far from being shy and reserved as you could get, but getting off with the chance of being seen hadn't been something I was into.

Or so I thought.

But then again this was Gage, and no one had ever been able to push my buttons like he could.

"Oh." I sighed when his fingers brushed over the front of my underwear effectively stopping my thoughts dead in their tracks. And when he gently brushed them back and forth, I dug my fingers into the wood and desperately tried to swallow the moan that wanted out.

I was rather unfamiliar with this needy version of myself. This woman who was two seconds away from begging a man to spin her around and just fuck her already.

Gage flattened his hand, pressing his palm right where I ached the most. I tried to move my hips, to create the friction I so desperately craved but he held me still. "Tell me you want me." I didn't know how it was possible but his voice was even lower.

My entire body lit up like I was standing in a puddle of live wires. Electricity zipping and zapping through my veins making my heart pump two times too fast. Given our position, I wasn't entirely sure how I managed it but I spun around and looked straight into his eyes.

"I do want you. Over me. Under me. *Inside* me. I don't care, Gage. I just want *you*."

Something sparked in his gaze. The intensity of it burning me to the soles of my feet. Then his mouth was on mine. Kissing me with so much hunger, so much ferocity it just about stole the breath from my lungs.

And still, it wasn't enough.

I reached between us and cupped him through his jeans. The sound he made when I did was one I could easily become addicted to. That was why I squeezed harder just so I could hear it again.

Somewhere between the kissing and groping, he'd managed to slip his hand under my dress again. Another one of those needy moans filled the air when his finger pushed past the barrier of my underwear.

"Shit Frankie, you're so damn wet."

Flexing my hips, I shamelessly rubbed myself against his hand. "And what are you going to do about it?"

Gage pulled my bottom lip between his teeth and gave it a little nibble. "That mouth." Applying more pressure, he dragged his fingers up and down. As good as it felt, I seriously needed him to do more before I took over and did it myself.

I was about to say as much when he suddenly pulled away and started unbuttoning his shirt. One button popped then another before his intense gaze was on me. "Take off your panties."

He did not have to tell me twice, I reached under my dress and slid the silky material down my legs before he got to the last button of his shirt and dropped it to the floor. When his jeans were out of the way too, Gage stepped forward, all hot and gloriously naked, and invaded my space again.

I didn't waste any time, smoothing my hands over the hard planes of his chest. He shivered at my touch and I simply couldn't resist getting a taste of him. Brushing my lips over his collarbone and down to his pec while he fumbled with the packet he'd pulled out of his wallet before he'd dropped his pants. His skin was warm and his scent so damn delicious.

Once we were both protected, he dragged his thumb along my jaw and guided my gaze back to his. I didn't know how long we stood there staring at each other. Could have been seconds. Could have been minutes. The world simply melted away, and I found myself drowning in the mossy depths of his eyes.

His thumb moved over my cheekbone in a featherlight touch before skittering over my jaw and finally tracing my bottom lip. I opened my mouth and flicked my tongue against the pad of his thumb, loving the way his eyes darkened.

His other hand moved up along my thigh, guiding my leg around his waist. Fingers digging into my skin, Gage leaned forward and whispered against my mouth, “I’ve never stopped wanting you.”

In the next second, he bent his knees slightly and pushed up into me in one swift motion. My breath caught. He groaned and muttered a curse. Then he moved. And oh did he move. Fast and hard, pushing me toward that blissful edge in no time at all.

“Mmm,” I moaned. Wanting to give myself over to the sensations coursing through my body, I closed my eyes and rolled my head back against the door. My little moment of bliss quickly cut short when Gage immediately stopped moving.

Lifting my head, I snapped my eyes open. His face was right there, mere inches from mine, eyes searching, mouth curved into a sexy smirk that made his dimple pop. I wiggled my hips, desperately needing him to move but instead of doing that, he pushed his hips forward and pinned me in place.

My heart flipped at the way he was looking at me. Like I was something precious, something to be worshipped. It made me feel both excited and scared at the same time.

I tried to wiggle my hips again. "You have to move or did you forget how this works?"

His smirk widened, a chuckle blowing over his lips. "So damn feisty." He inched closer still. "I fucking love it."

Then his mouth was on mine in one of those searing kisses that turned my blood to lava, and easily stole the words from my tongue and replaced it with an intoxicating hunger for more of him. His lips continued to move over mine, his rhythm slow yet brutal. Taking, giving and then taking some more. I wanted to yell and scream but mostly I wanted to stay lost in that moment forever.

And just when I thought it couldn't possibly get any better, his hips finally moved again. Matching the rhythm of his soul-stealing kiss, he slowly moved in and out of me. Branding me, ruining me with every thrust of his hips and lick of his tongue.

It was driving me insane.

He was driving me insane.

Everything felt electric. Magnified. My skin was hot, too hot, and yet I was covered in goosebumps from head to toe. Low, low in my belly was an insistent tug screaming that I needed more.

So so much more.

Curving my hands over his shoulders, I dug my nails into his skin and managed to tear my mouth from his. "Faster." The word huffed out in a breathless plea.

In answer, his thrusting slowed down even more. His mouth coasting over the skin of my neck like he was committing every inch to memory. He smoothed his hand up my side, his thumb only just touching the underside of my breast.

"I want you to feel *everything*." Gage traced a path around my breast slowly working his way to the tip. "Pleasure like this should be unhurried. Savored." He continued with his barely-there touch on my breast while his hips kept rocking to a torturously slow rhythm. "It should be drawn out and made to last."

My fingers dug even deeper, and I wanted to yell at him, demand him to take me faster, harder. Then it happened. One thrust. Two thrusts. Three thrusts and my world shattered. Back arching off the door, I felt the orgasm ripple through my body in a tidal wave of pleasure.

Pleasure so intense, it threatened to rip me apart.

"Yes," he breathed into my ear. "Come for me, Frankie."

As I continued to experience sensations I never knew existed, it didn't take Gage all that long to follow me. Burying his face in the crook of my neck, he whispered my name as the dam broke for him.

We were still breathing hard when he lifted his head and cradled my face between his palms. I swallowed hard at the intensity in his gaze and even harder when his lips parted to speak, "I—"

I'd never know what he meant to say because instead of talking he kissed me. Although there was nothing sexual about it, it still set me on fire. In a different way, though. I couldn't really explain it but it was almost like he was trying to convey with his kiss what he couldn't with his words.

It was also very possible that my orgasm brain was the one doing the thinking at that very moment. Which was exactly why I didn't pay too much attention to it, choosing to focus on the delicious way Gage's mouth moved over mine.

When we finally pulled apart after who knew how long, he brushed a few strands of hair out my face. "That was not at all how I wanted this to go."

"Oh yeah?"

"Mhm." His eyes tracked the movement of his finger brushing over the collar of my dress. "I didn't even get to see you naked."

A laugh bubbled through me. "Well, the night is still young. Play your cards right and you might just get lucky." His eyebrow slowly quirked prompting me to add, "Again."

Grinning, he traced the swell of my breast. "I like the sound of that." He looked down between us before meeting my gaze again. "I have to take care of this." Touching his mouth to mine, he kissed me far too quickly before dragging his pants up and heading toward the bathroom.

As I watched him leave, I wasn't all too shocked when my brain warned me things would never be the same after this. What did manage to ruffle me was the realization that even though the heart was an organ it also retained muscle memory. Because everything I thought I didn't feel for this man anymore was still there. Sitting dormant in a locked space in my heart that only he had the key to.

And now that he'd unlocked it, and my heart lay vulnerable at his feet, I could only hope history wouldn't repeat itself.

26

GAGE

"We never had dessert."

Frankie looked to where I was standing in the entryway of her kitchen. "Uhm."

Shaking my head, I pushed off the frame and started walking toward her. "Not *that* kind. The kind you eat with your mouth." She rolled her lips inward, desperately trying—and failing—to keep her smile at bay.

Shit, I loved this look on her. This casual no walls up look. It made my heart do funny things and my head think things it really shouldn't. Things like how I could get used to seeing her like this every damn day of my life.

Picking up my pace, I closed the distance between us and sidled in behind her. I brushed my nose along the shell of her ear and snaked my arm around her waist. Tugging her close, I spoke low. "Such a dirty mind." I nipped on her skin. "What will I ever do with you?"

Mastered in the art of driving me out of my damn mind, Frankie pushed her ass back and glanced at me over her shoulder. "That's a very good question." Her gaze shot to my mouth. "What will you do?"

She wasn't even done talking when I gripped her hips and pulled her even more flush against me, leaving her with zero doubts as to how her little performance was affecting me. I leaned forward and pressed a kiss against her shoulder.

"I have a few ideas," I told her. "And I'll show you…after I've sampled a few of your brownies."

Frankie's brows drew together. "You want brownies? Now?"

"Yes, now. My mouth has been watering for your brownies almost as much as it has been watering over you."

Her smile spread wide as she turned around and smoothed her hand up my bare chest. It was insane how big of an effect that little skin-to-skin contact had on me. How every nerve ending in my body suddenly felt alive and on fire.

"Guess I better get you your fix then." Frankie's eyes flicked to my mouth before settling on mine again. She inched closer and closer until her lips brushed over my neck. I sucked in a sharp breath and dug my fingers into her hips. "But you're helping."

She pulled back and side-stepped out of my grasp so fast I didn't even have time to react. In fact, by the time my brain caught up with everything she was on the other side of the kitchen placing ingredients on the counter.

Chuckling, I dragged my hand through my hair and walked over to where she was. When I reached her Frankie pushed a bowl with butter toward me. "Grab a pot and melt that."

Lifting the corner of my mouth into a half-grin, I pressed two fingers against my temple in a salute. "Yes, ma'am."

While I melted the butter over the stove, I couldn't help but steal a few glances at Frankie. She was sifting flour and cocoa into a bowl, and I could tell by the look on her face that her mind was somewhere else.

I'd hoped to calm some of her doubts but now I was afraid that by admitting the truth I might've made her even more cautious of me…of us. If that was the case, I would just have to work twice as hard to convince her I wasn't going anywhere anytime soon.

With that thought in mind, I grabbed a kitchen towel before I took the melted butter back to Frankie. I poured it over the sugar and just watched her as she went about mixing everything together.

When a worried look still marred her features a few minutes later, I couldn't take it anymore and simply had to know. "What are you thinking about?" I dipped my finger in the barely mixed batter and Frankie immediately swatted my hand.

Giving me a playful side-eye, she moved the mixing bowl out of my reach and continued to gently stir. "After you left I made a point of leaving the room whenever someone mentioned your name so I never really knew what was happening in your life. I'm just curious, I guess."

"Curious huh? About what exactly?" I bumped her shoulder with mine. "Other women maybe?"

The look she gave me had me cupping my balls on instinct until her face lit up with amusement. "I don't care about those. What I really wondered about was why you left the fire department and went into business with my brother. For as long as I'd known you, you'd wanted to be a firefighter so when Caden told our parents that the two of you were starting (Construction Name) I was stunned."

I watched her pull a buttered dish closer and dump the chocolate mix into it. Even though this particular event lived with me every day of my life, I couldn't remember the last time I'd told it to anyone.

Nan didn't even know about it.

"I think almost every firefighter I've met has a story similar to this," I started. "The one where you run into a burning building with your brother and only one of you make it out."

Sliding the dish into the oven, Frankie set the timer before turning to face me. She didn't say anything, simply waited patiently for me to continue.

"Jonah was my mentor. He'd taken me under his wing from the first day I walked into the station and I'd come to see him as a second father. He was one of the greatest people I'd ever met but stubborn as a damn mule.

Everything that day happened so fast. One moment he was arguing with the chief about coming out of the building when there could still be people inside and in the next he was buried beneath the caved-in roof." I leaned my ass against the counter and rested my elbows on the surface. "We always knew the risks. Knew how ruthless a fire could be but no amount of training could have ever prepared us for the moment the worst happened."

I shook my head, that feeling of helplessness I'd felt that day buzzing below the surface of my skin. "The thing that really got me was how it affected his family. How they fell apart at his funeral. His wife had held on to the casket like it was her lifeline. It broke my heart and all I could think about was my nan and how it would destroy her if something like that happened to me."

Frankie moved across the room, pressing her palms against my cheeks when she reached me. "I'm sorry. For you and for his family."

I curled my fingers around her hands and dragged first her left then her right wrist to my mouth. Guiding her arms around my waist, I held her close as I spoke into her hair. "I didn't want to cause anyone I loved that kind of hurt so I decided to walk away from something that called to the very bottom of my soul.

Of course, your brother wasn't going to let me wallow in self-pity. It took him an afternoon to come up with the concept of Blue Ladder Construction and since I knew my way around a building site thanks to my dad and I still had my inheritance sitting untouched, I figured why not."

Frankie studied me with those big beautiful blue eyes, the intensity of her stare cutting a path straight to my soul. What did she see when she looked at me like that? I was about to ask when she took my face in her hands and pressed her mouth to mine in a tender kiss.

One that touched every fiber of my being. One that warned me it would be impossible to ever let this woman go.

Before I had time to deepen it though an annoying sound sliced through the air. It was only when Frankie pulled away and hurried to the oven that I realized the brownies were done.

Grabbing her oven mitts, she quickly pulled them out and set the pan on a rack. She lifted her head, meeting my gaze as I slowly stalked toward her. "They need to cool off before you can eat them."

"You're gonna have to find some other way to occupy my mouth until then."

With a smile of pure sin touching her lips, she spun around and reached behind her neck before she fiddled with the side of her dress. Not even a second later, the fabric split open and the material bunched around her feet.

My feet faltered, my breath catching in my throat. Because holy shit the sight of Frankie standing before me in nothing but a lace g-string and heels was enough to almost bring me to my knees.

Actually, that's exactly where I wanted to be: On my knees in front of her.

Moving fast, I closed the distance between us. The second I was able to, I trailed my fingertips along her collarbone to the hollow of her throat. From there I brushed them down the center of her chest before slowly tracing the outline of one perfect breast.

Frankie sucked in a sharp breath. I continued my slow torture until I couldn't stand it anymore and simply had to bend down and suck the tip into my mouth.

"Oh." She sighed. "That feels so good." Her fingers slipped into my hair, the tips digging into my scalp while her other hand came up to squeeze the breast that wasn't in my mouth.

The way she wasn't afraid to take charge of her own pleasure drove me out of my damn mind. It was so hot. So sexy. I was half-tempted to step back and tell her to put on a show for me.

I probably would have done just that if the ache between my legs hadn't made itself known. Needing to bury myself inside this woman yet again, I gripped her hips and made a move to lift her onto the counter.

But knowing Frankie and how she felt about her kitchen, I carried her to the living room instead. Setting her down on the edge of the couch, I kneeled between her legs. I brushed my fingers over her underwear. "As sexy as this is, it needs to go."

Hooking my fingers in the waistband, I pulled the fabric down her legs and tossed it to the side. Gently smoothing my hands up her thighs, I guided her legs over my shoulders. I leaned forward, scraping my teeth over her hipbone.

She shivered and rocked her hips. "So impatient," I breathed as I moved to the opposite side and did the same. "So needy."

"Gage, please?"

My tongue darted out, just barely touching her sensitive skin. "What do you want?"

"Your mouth," she begged, her voice all sexy and breathy. "I want your mouth on me...now."

Gripping her hips, I buried my face between her thighs and almost groaned when that first taste of her hit my tongue. Sweet and addictive. So damn addictive. I licked and sucked, eagerly lapping up everything she had to give, while Frankie writhed with reckless abandon.

Threading her fingers through my hair, she arched her back off the couch and moaned. "Yes. Oh, yes."

Knowing I had this effect on her drove me absolutely insane. It was like a high I'd never known and shit, the only way I wanted to come down was by being buried balls deep inside while she came with my name on her tongue.

With that thought and a great deal of effort, I lifted my head and stood. Frankie's confused gaze slammed into me almost immediately. Fishing out my wallet, I jerked my head toward the couch she was sitting on.

"Bend over."

Her smile was so damn sexy when she slowly slipped off the couch, turned around, and bent over it. Looking at me over her shoulder, she arched her back and pushed her ass out like an offering.

An offering I was so eager to take, I fumbled with the little square packet before finally rolling the condom on. I was on my knees behind her not even a second later.

I smoothed my hand up her spine until I could slip my fingers into her hair. With one hand resting on her hip, I rocked forward and lost myself to the tight warmth of her. Her body wrapped so tight around me felt incredible…and right.

Like my body had been made just to fit hers. Like she was mine.

Mine.

It was that thought that drove my hips forward again and again. Thrusting in and out of her with hard and fast movements. Movements that seemed to drive her as crazy as it did me.

"Oh yes, Gage, just like that."

My fingers in her hair tightened as I leaned over her and growled in her ear, "You like it when I fuck you hard."

"Mmm," she moaned. "Yes."

Her breathy little moans were like the sweetest melody to my ears only rivaled by the sound of the husky way she whispered my name when her body shuddered around me. Needing to be right there with her, I picked up my pace until my world finally exploded.

Dropping my head to her shoulder, I spoke against her clammy skin, "You're mine now and I'm not letting you go."

27

FRANKIE

"I can't remember the last time I saw you smile like this."

Tearing my eyes away from where Maia was helping my mom with the dessert, I looked at my dad. "What are you talking about? I always smile."

His gaze flicked to the kitchen before meeting mine again. "This one seems…different. Bigger. Brighter."

Pretty sure a week of amazing monkey sex would do that to you. But I couldn't tell my dad that, so I just shrugged and went with, "I have no idea what you're talking about."

Shifting to the edge of the couch, he leaned forward and tapped me on the knee. "Your mom and I are deliriously happy about this new development. It's been a *looong* time coming."

Eyes still trained on me, he made himself comfortable again. "As happy as I am for you, kiddo, I have to ask: Are you prepared for this little instant family you're getting?"

Once again, my gaze flicked to Maia. Brows pinched together, she was typing something on her phone—which now that I thought about it, she'd been doing a lot more than usual, although she could very well have been talking with her dad since he had a shift at the station.

Once she was done, she slipped the device into her pocket and lifted her head. Our eyes met and her lips instantly curved into a smile. A feeling of rightness rushed over me. Like this was how everything was supposed to be.

I turned my attention back to my dad. "Prepared? Probably not. But if you're asking me whether I'm sure I really want this, the answer is one hundred percent yes. And I know it's all still so new and none of us know what the future might bring, but for right now I'm happy."

My dad smiled one of those big smiles he always graced me with when I'd done something to make him proud. "And that's enough for me. All I ever wanted was for my kids to be happy, no matter what that looked like to them."

Blinking away the sudden sting behind my eyes, I said, "Love you, Dad."

"I love you right back, kiddo."

Mom and Maia joined us a few moments later and as always Mom's (dessert name) went down a treat. And so did Mom and Dad's tales of how naughty Caden and Gage were as teenage boys.

They even pulled out the photo albums and much to my horror showed Maia every possible embarrassing photo they could find. I didn't mind too much, not when Maia looked so happy and especially not when my parents were so amazing with her.

By the time we'd worked through two albums, we had to say goodbye since I didn't want Maia to get to bed too late. Our ride was made in silence since Maia was on the phone for most of it.

I found it a bit odd but didn't say anything. It was only after I prepared hot chocolate and saw her on the phone yet again when I walked into the living room that I piped up.

"Alright, Asgardian, that thing has been glued to your hand almost all night." I set our mugs on the coffee table before sinking into the couch adjacent to Maia's. "And judging by that smile on your face, I'm guessing it's a boy on the other end."

Maia's nose wrinkled with disgust. "Ew, no it's not a boy."

"Oookay, a girl then?"

She shook her head. "No, it's…it's…" Huffing out a sigh way too heavy for a kid her age, she pulled her lip between her teeth and stared at the phone still clutched in her hand.

"Hey." I reached across and tapped her arm. Waiting until she trained those big brown eyes on me, I spoke, "You don't have to tell me anything you don't want, okay? I was just being a nosy so and so because I'm not used to you being on your phone."

"It's my mom." The words came flying out of her mouth and if her wide eyes and suddenly pale cheeks were anything to go by, I would have bet my life she wanted to take them back.

I didn't understand why, though. "Isn't that a good thing?"

Maia's brows furrowed. "Dad hasn't talked to you about her…or me?"

"Your dad talks about you a lot, Maia. But it's always to tell me how wonderful you are and how proud he is of you. We haven't talked about your past if that's what you're asking."

Chewing on her lip again, her gaze frantically bounced between me and her phone like she couldn't decide where attention needed to be. She was nervous. The air practically buzzed with the tension she was emitting.

And just when I wanted to reassure her that she didn't have to tell me anything she finally spoke. "My mom isn't—wasn't—a very good person. She did bad things and because of those bad things I was taken away from her."

Her voice wobbled and I couldn't stop myself from jumping up. Sitting on the armrest of her chair, I wrapped my arms around her shoulders and pulled her tight to me. My heart squeezed something fierce when she hugged me right back.

We sat like that until she was comfortable enough to pull away and speak again, "She was always in and out of jail or rehab and every time she'd get clean and promise we'd be together again."

She shook her head. "I'm not stupid, I can see the patterns too. But deep down I believe that one day she really will get clean and stay clean." Turning her head, she focused on a spot on the wall for the longest time.

When the silence between us became almost too much to handle, she finally spoke again. "Dad once told me that people get their strength from other people believing in them. Maybe if I keep believing in her, she'll finally get better, and we can be together again."

My heart started beating faster. "Do you…do you not want to live with your dad anymore?" I could barely say the words, they felt thick and scratchy coming up my throat.

"No!" Maia's gaze smashed into mine, those beautiful eyes looking almost bewildered. "I mean I don't want to leave my dad ever but…" her eyes filled tears, and I had to swallow down hard to keep my own emotions in check. "She's still my mom."

Those four words fell from her lips soft and broken. My heart shattered into a million pieces for this little girl. For everything she went through and everything she felt she needed to carry on her shoulders.

I pulled her in for another hug, wishing like hell I could absorb everything bad she was feeling.

"Frankie?"

"Yeah?"

She looked up at me, eyes almost pleading. "Please don't tell Dad I'm talking to my mom. He won't understand."

"Oh, Maia. I can't—"

"I promise I'll tell him. I'm just waiting until after Nan's surgery because I know how stressed he is, and I don't want to add to that."

I didn't like it, but she was right about Gage being worried about his grandma and honestly, I had no idea what this news of Maia's mom would do to him. But I also didn't want to keep secrets from him. Nor did I want to lose this relationship I was building with Maia.

I took her face in my hands. "We shouldn't keep things from your dad." She started to pull away, so I quickly sputtered out the rest of my words, hoping like hell I was doing the right thing. "We can wait until the surgery is done then you and I will tell him together, okay?"

Her arms were around me not even a second later, hugging me tight. This time I was unable to swallow down the lump in my throat or blink away the sting behind my eyes. It was a little scary how fast this girl had crawled into my heart.

We pulled apart after I didn't even know how long. Eyes red, cheeks blotchy, she said her goodnights and disappeared up the stairs.

I was still sitting on the armrest wrestling with my emotions long after she went to bed. I didn't want to lie to Gage. I didn't want any secrets between us. But I also wanted to protect Maia.

Later that night when I finally crawled into bed, I had this sinking feeling that I was about to lose someone's trust. I just didn't know if it was going to be Gage's or Maia's.

28

GAGE

Amazing how fast things could change.

A little over three weeks ago everything had felt off-balance, out of control. I'd wondered how I was going to apologize to Frankie and get her back. I'd been stressed out of my mind about how unhappy Maia seemed to be and had seriously doubted whether I was really equipped to raise a daughter.

And now here I was.

Sitting on the beach with Frankie tucked against me while we watched Maia play at the shoreline. Hair whipping in every which way, her happy laughter carrying on the wind, she was chasing the waves as they crashed down on the sand.

My heart couldn't take it.

"Hey," Frankie said. Twisting her body, she pressed her hand against my chest and peered up at me. "Can I ask you something?"

There was something about the tone of her voice that had an uneasy feeling coasting down my spine. Pushing it away, I tucked a few wayward strands behind her ear, gently stroking her cheek with my thumb.

"You know you can ask me anything."

Frankie nodded, but it was the hard swallow she worked down that gave me pause. That uneasy was back in tenfold. “Maia’s mom…where is she?”

For as often as I talked about Maia with Frankie, I’d never told her how Maia ended up in the system. Mostly because it never came up but if I were being completely honest it was also because some part of me didn’t want to tell her.

Not because I was ashamed. I simply didn’t want Kim Lín tainting anything else in our lives.

“Maia’s mom is a piece of work.” My gaze drifted to where she was happily running around. “An addict. She’s been in and out of Maia’s life too many times to count. Every time she claims to be clean and just as Maia thinks she has her mom back; the woman chooses drugs over her daughter and splits.”

I shook my head, disgust and bile burning up the inside of my throat. “About seven months ago Mrs. Reiner and I thought it would be okay for Maia to start spending time with her mom again. Kim had sworn up and down that she was clean and getting the help she needed.

I should have known it was all a load of bullshit. On the day that was supposed to be her third visit with her mom, Maia found her flat on her face almost drowning in her own sick, needle still sticking out of her arm. That poor kid had to call 911 and go to the hospital with her mom’s sorry ass.” I gritted my teeth. “That poor kid had been so traumatized. She never should have gone through that.”

Frankie’s sharp intake of breath had me turning my attention to her again. Eyes taking up almost half of her face, she’d gone completely pale. “That’s why she’s not in Maia’s life?”

"Kind of, yeah." I ran my hand through my hair. "The last time Maia saw Kim she was in the hospital going through the stages of withdrawal. It hadn't been pretty." My heart squeezed painfully tight as I remembered how broken and devastated Maia had been.

"Mrs. Reiner told Kim if she ever wanted some sort of contact with Maia again she needed to get clean and stay clean. She's been at some rehabilitation facility since. While she's there Mrs. Reiner and I thought it best to cut off all communication between them."

"So they're not allowed to communicate with each other?" Frankie curled her hand around her throat, her already pale skin looking even paler. "At all?"

I shrugged. "Rationally, I know I can't keep them apart forever and I don't want to either. I just want to give Maia some time. Time to find herself and time for her heart to heal. She can't handle another rejection from that woman right now."

Frankie looked like she wanted to throw up. Hand pressed against her stomach, her gaze shot to Maia for the longest time before meeting mine again. Her lips trembled as the words tumbled out of her mouth. "I'm so sorry. I…I didn't know."

I took her face in my hands. "You have nothing to be sorry for besides it's all good. Just look at how happy Maia finally is. With every day that passes her heart is mending."

Frankie's eyes glistened as they frantically bounced between mine. She was scaring me a little. "Are you okay?"

Again, she swallowed hard. Her mouth opened and closed several times before she finally said, "I don't feel so good. I think it's something I ate."

That uneasy feeling from before was back again because for whatever reason Frankie was lying to me.

29

FRANKIE

That awful feeling in the pit of my stomach never went away. I wasn't sure if it was there because of what I'd learned or because I had the chance to tell Gage the truth and chose to lie instead.

Thankfully his grandma's surgery was today and hopefully that meant Maia and I could come out with the truth later tonight. Because I sure as shit needed this dark spot to come into the light. And with any luck, Gage wouldn't be too upset with us.

Knowing how he felt about Maia's mom, I highly doubted that.

"Well?" Caden's voice filtered through my thoughts and forced me back to the present.

Standing in place, I did a slow three-sixty, taking in my gorgeous new kitchen. I could hardly believe this was the very same kitchen that'd been nothing but soot and rubble a few short weeks ago.

Facing him where he was standing with his shoulder propped against the frame. I grinned at him. "It looks amazing."

"I'm glad you think so." Straightening, he trailed behind me as I swept my fingertips over the shiny stainless-steel counters. "It won't be that long before Sugar Booger is open for business again."

I stopped at one of the ovens and opened it to look inside. There weren't many things that got me as excited as shiny new appliances. My fingers were already itching to knead some dough and make a few batches of cinnamon rolls.

Closing the oven again, I turned to face my brother. "Thank you doesn't even come close. For this and for getting me that meeting with James Meuser. He offered me a pretty sweet deal."

"You're very, very welcome." His face lit up with pride and that all-too-familiar mushy feeling coated my insides. "Although I think your gratitude should be aimed at Gage and the guys." He chuckled. "Or maybe just the guys since they had to put up with Gage busting their balls to get everything done perfectly."

Heat crept up my neck and settled in my cheeks. It wasn't embarrassment but rather that warm ooey-gooey feeling I got whenever Gage looked at me. It made me feel—dare I say it?—loved.

Would he still look at me like that when he learns the truth?

"If that goofy look on your face is anything to go by, I take it things are going good between the two of you?"

"Yeah." I nibbled on my lip and tried to calm the swooshing inside my stomach before it bottomed out. "It's going really, really great."

Caden sidled in beside me and wrapped an arm around my shoulders. “Then why do you look worried right now?”

Crap, I didn’t think he’d notice.

“If he’s not treating you—”

“He’s perfect, Caden.” I tilted my head to look at him. “So is Maia. And I can’t imagine a day without either of them in my life. That’s the problem. It’s too soon for any of these feelings to be taking root inside me.”

“Is it though?” Stepping back, he leaned his butt against the counter. Ducking his head, he made sure to look directly into my eyes when he spoke. “You’ve loved him for years, Frankie. Maybe you’re just admitting it to yourself now, but it’s always been there.”

He was right. My feelings for Gage never went away, I just buried them in some untouchable corner of my heart. And now there was another person who’d forever hold a piece of my heart too.

Maybe if I was really lucky, I’d get to keep them both.

Smiling, I flicked my wrist to check the time. “Oh shoot, I’ve gotta go. Gage’s grandma is going in for her surgery today and I’m supposed to meet him and Maia at the hospital in ten minutes.” I hugged my brother and gave him a quick peck on the cheek. “The bakery looks amazing.”

I rushed to my car and drove to the hospital as fast as the speed limit would allow. By the time I walked up to the main entrance Gage and Maia were already there. Standing with their backs to me, they had their eyes glued to the parking area.

“I’m not that late, am I?”

They both spun around to face me, eyes lighting up and smiles spreading wide. Gosh, it made me feel all sorts of things. But what really did me in was when Maia sprinted toward me and wrapped me up in the tightest hug.

Emotion burned up my throat and settled behind my eyes as I hugged her right back. It didn't matter that I'd only known her for a little while or that she wasn't even really mine, not biologically at least.

None of it mattered because when it came down to it, I knew without a single ounce of doubt that I loved this girl like she was my own and I would do absolutely anything to protect her.

"Oh you've done it now," I told her when she pulled back. "From now on that's how I expect to be greeted."

The grin on her face could light up a freaking room. "Deal."

I took her hand and after receiving a way to quick kiss from Gage we made our way to his grandma's room. I could only laugh when we walked in on her studying her roots in a little hand mirror with a scowl on her face.

"The first thing I'm doing once I get out of here is seeing Macy. My hair looks even worse than Ethel's three rooms down." She set the mirror on the bed and leaned forward with her hand cupping her mouth. "And that's saying a lot since her hair looks like a monkey's ass."

"Nan!"

Mrs. Calloway rolled her eyes. "Butt. Monkey's butt. Gosh, you'd think all the bed gymnastics you're doing would loosen you up a bit."

Parking his hands on his hips, Gage groaned and dropped his chin to his chest while Maia and I desperately tried not to laugh.

Shaking her head, Mrs. Calloway turned her attention to me. "I have a surefire way of removing the stick from any man's *butt*. You take your finger and you—"

"Seriously, Nan! Maia is right here!"

Not even fazed by his admonishment, she winked at me. "I'll tell you later when mr-stick-up-his-butt isn't here. Trust me, you'll thank me." She gave him a pointed stare. "You both will."

Never in all the years I'd known this man had I seen his cheeks turn that particular shade of red. Even his ears were glowing. It was very difficult not to pull my phone out of my pocket and snap a picture.

Gage's grandma didn't share my restraint. Pulling her phone from who the heck knew where she aimed it at Gage. He was in the process of lifting his hand toward it when the shutter sound rang through the room.

Grinning like she'd just won the lottery; Gage's grandma studied the screen before showing it to him. "Red is not a good color on you at all."

He opened his mouth but before a single word sounded, a doctor came waltzing in. "Alright, Mrs. Calloway are you ready for me?" He looked around the room and after introducing himself as Gage's grandma's surgeon, he began explaining the procedure.

The more he talked, the paler Gage's face became. Slipping in beside him, I laced my fingers through his and leaned in close. "Hey, I'm here."

Our eyes met, and he squeezed my hand. I wasn't prepared for what I saw swirling in those green irises. Everything I felt for this man was right there staring back at me and I knew he loved me right back.

Even if he didn't quite know it yet.

"I'll take good care of her." The doctor tapped Gage's shoulder before leaving the room.

"See? I told you there was nothing to worry about," Mrs. surname said.

Gage gave my hand one more squeeze before releasing it to go sit on his grandma's bed. "I'll always worry about you, Nan."

Her eyes glistened as she reached forward and took his face in her hands. "And I love you for it."

Maia moved across the room and slipped her arm around my waist just as a nurse walked in. "Oki doki, Mrs. Calloway, let's get you ready to go." She turned to us. "You can wait in the waiting room and I will come let you know the moment she is out of surgery."

One and a half hours later, we were informed that Mrs. Calloway's surgery was done without any complications. As great as that news was, all three of us only breathed a sigh of relief once she was wheeled out of the recovery room another hour later.

Because she was still groggy from the anesthesia and needed her rest, we didn't spend too much time hanging around. Once we were certain she was okay—well as okay as she could be after major surgery—we decided to head home.

"I don't know about you guys, but I am starved," Gage said as we walked through the front lobby. "Maybe we could—"

He immediately stopped walking, his body tense as he stared at something in the distance. I followed his gaze, his low angry words reaching my ears just as my eyes landed on a willowy woman walking toward us. "What the fuck is she doing here?"

30

FRANKIE

You didn't have to be a genius to know the woman slinking toward us was Maia's mom or that the proverbial shit was about to hit the freaking fan.

Sucking in a breath, I curled my hand around Gage's bicep and tried to pull him closer to me. "Gage, you—"

"How the hell did she find us?" he growled.

I had a pretty good idea and all it took was one look at Maia's pale face for me to know I was right.

Shit.

Shit, shit, shit.

My gaze flicked to the woman—who was closing in on us with rapid speed—before landing on Maia again. She looked so frail and out of place. Like she wanted to melt into the nearest wall and disappear.

I need to protect her.

The words rolled around in my head loud and clear. It wasn't that I was afraid of what Gage might do if he knew it was Maia who led her here. Because I wasn't. I knew the last thing he'd ever want to do was hurt Maia in any way.

Just like I knew the anger running through his veins right now had the ability to hurt their relationship. And I couldn't allow that to happen.

"It was me," I blurted out.

Yeah, so maybe this wasn't the way to teach a young impressionable girl how to take responsibility for her actions. It was the only way I knew how to protect her though.

Gage's eyes cut to mine, so angry, so hurt I felt my heart break a little. "What did you say?"

"Dad, she's—"

"No!" Looking at Maia, I shook my head slightly and wordlessly begged her to let me do this. She stared at me for a long, long moment before slowly opening her mouth. Even though I knew I should, some part of me just couldn't stand back and do nothing.

"I found her and we've been texting back and forth."

Anyone who wasn't blinded by rage could see the holes in my story from a mile away. How would I even know how to get in contact with anyone from their past. And more importantly, why would I do it.

But Gage was so very angry, those thoughts never crossed his mind. Which was a good thing in that moment because it bought Maia some time. To what exactly, I didn't know.

"Why the fuck did you do that?" He took a step closer, and I almost flinched at the look on his face. "Didn't I tell what that woman did to Maia? Don't you care that *my daughter* could get hurt?"

I do care! So much.

"I'm sorry, I didn't think—"

"Yeah." He closed his eyes and pinched the bridge of his nose. When his lids parted, I saw nothing but coldness staring back at me. "You didn't fucking think. I can't believe you did this." He shook his head. "I can't even look at you right now."

Spinning around, he took Maia's hand. "We're going home."

"Dad, please, I want—"

"Not now, Maia."

She looked at me over her shoulder and I swear I felt my heart shatter into a million pieces. I'd just taken her voice from her. Instead of letting her stand on her own two feet and speak her mind, I stepped in and tried to save a situation that didn't need saving.

Not only that, but I also managed to ruin everything good in my life in the process too. I brushed my fingers over the spot inside my chest that hurt something fierce, my eyes glued to the two people I loved so dearly.

Was I supposed to run after them?

Or wait until the situation calmed?

Shit. I didn't know what to do.

I was still staring when I felt someone next to me. Blinking away the tears stinging in the back of my eyes, I angled my head to the side. Maia's mom stood nibbling on her lip with her hands clasped in front of her.

A few inches shorter than me with her inky hair pulled away from her face in a ponytail and dark smudges under her eyes, I had trouble reconciling her with Maia. This woman looked frail and fragile where Maia was fierce and strong.

She cautiously lifted her hand. "My name is Kim, I'm Maia's mom."

"I know who you are." The bite in my tone had nothing to do with anything that'd just happened and everything with how this woman had treated her daughter. I didn't even care that I had no right to be angry on Maia's behalf because as far as I was concerned when you cared about someone, you cared about how people treated them.

"I'm sorry," she said. "I guess the scene was because of me?"

I rubbed my forehead. "Something like that."

"I…uh…" She sucked in a breath, her gaze flicking to the exit. "I thought it would be fine, you know? Maia said Gage was okay with me and her texting. When she mentioned his grandma's surgery, I wanted to…I don't know…offer support."

Why the hell was she telling me any of this? Ugh, it made my brain hurt.

"You're Frankie, right?"

"What?"

"Maia sent me a picture of the two of you in a kitchen. You were teaching her how to bake."

Throb. Throb. Throb. My brain slammed against my skull. I tried to think, to do anything but see the look on Maia and Gage's faces before they left. One hurt, one angry, and I'd put it there.

I needed to talk to someone. Not just anyone but the one person I trusted most. But first I had a few things to say to *Kim*.

"Look," I started. "I don't know why you're here now or what you're hoping to accomplish. All I know is that Maia is an amazing kid. She's overcome so much and grown into a girl I would be proud to call my own. But beneath her wonder woman exterior, she's still a little girl who can get hurt in the blink of an eye.

"I can't tell you what to do but I am begging you if you being in her life is something temporary please, *please* walk away. She doesn't deserve to be hurt again. And if you want a relationship with her then show her she's worth fighting for."

Whatever response she had; I didn't want to hear it. Turning on my heel, I got the hell out of there as fast as I could.

Ten minutes later, I was standing on Maddie's porch tapping my knuckles against the door. When it creaked open after a few moments, I immediately lunged forward and threw my arms around my best friend.

"Hey, what happened?"

Those tears that'd been sitting on the cusp of falling finally slid down my cheeks, thick and hot. And once they started there was no stopping them.

Maddie's hand smoothed up my back. "Okay, you're scaring me. Did something happen to Gage's grandma?"

Not able to speak, I shook my head. My shaky "no," muffled against her shoulder.

Without saying a word, she ushered me inside and led me to the couch. I rested my elbows on my thighs and dropped my head into my hands. All of this felt so…stupid.

The couch dipped as Maddie took a seat next to me and gently set her hand on my shoulder. "Talk to me, Frankie. What's got you so upset?"

Lifting my head, I stared into the distance. "I made a mistake. I thought I was doing something good but I think I just ended up hurting Maia." Angling my head, I looked at Maddie and told her everything that'd happened.

When I was done, I fell back against the couch and threw my arm over my face. “I want to go over there but what if Maia doesn’t want to tell Gage the truth anymore? Won’t I just make it worse? I seriously don’t know what to do.”

“I think you should go.” Maddie smoothed her hands up and down her thighs. “You can’t build a relationship—whether it’s yours and Gage’s or Gage and Maia’s—on a foundation of secrets.”

“I know,” I breathed out as I pushed to my feet and pulled Maddie into a hug when she stood too. “Thank you, Maddie-Cakes.”

As I rushed to my car, I only hoped that a small misunderstanding wouldn’t cost me the two people I cared about most.

31

GAGE

Maia yanked her hand from mine. "Dad, will you stop walking for a second?"

Stopping in my tracks, I glanced at her. With her arms crossed in front of her and her brows pinched tight, she looked pissed…at me. Which I really didn't get because I wasn't the one texting with Kim.

Nope, that was all Frankie.

Shit. Just thinking it didn't feel right. There was this nagging feeling at the back of my head that I'd got it all wrong. But if not her then who…and how? My brain was still trying to piece everything together when I noticed Frankie coming out of the hospital.

Even though we were standing in the parking lot a good stretch away from the entrance, I could still see she was upset. Everything in me screamed to go to her, to at least hear her out.

Because I knew, I damn well knew Frankie would never do something unless she had a good reason for it.

"It was me." Maia's whispered words slammed into me with the force of a freight train.

I tore my eyes away from Frankie to look at Maia. "What?"

Those big brown eyes glistened with tears, her throat bobbing up and down with the swallow she worked down. "I don't know why Frankie said what she said. It was all me. I've been texting with my mom and I told her about Nan's surgery today. I didn't think she'd show up here."

There was a split second of complete and utter silence before the sound of my heart slamming against my ribs became almost deafening. I wanted to hide my head and cover my ears just to escape it for a few moments.

But there was no escaping this.

Heaving out a heavy breath, I dragged my palms over my face. "For how long?"

Maia shrugged. With her arms now wrapped around her waist, her stance had gone from defensive to protective. "A few weeks. One of my friends from the center helped me get her number."

She rolled her lip over her teeth a few times. "I didn't want to ask Mrs. NAME because I knew she'd tell you and…" she sucked in a deep breath, her next words falling from her lips whisper-soft, "I didn't want you to know."

My brain felt fuzzy, shaky. I was hearing the words, but I had a damn hard time believing them to be true. Still, I opened my mouth and words rolled off my tongue, "You didn't want me to know?"

Shaking her head, she gave me an incredulous look. "You hate my mom, and you keep telling me how you don't want her in my life."

Well, shit.

Taking two steps forward, I placed my hands on Maia's upper arms. "I don't hate your mom, Maia. I'm just angry about how you were treated. The only thing I hate is that you had to go through any of it."

Her eyes searched mine, and I saw wisdom far beyond her years shine in them. "But *I'm* not angry. And if you would have listened to me, you would've known that I don't want to leave you, I just want to get to know my mom."

She was crying now. Two streams of thick tears rolled down her cheeks and hit me right in the center of my heart. "As far as I am concerned," she went on, her voice wobbly. "You are my dad and don't want that to change. But you've told me before to always see the good in people and if I can't see the good in my mom, no one else will."

"Oh Maia," I wrapped my arms around her and held her close to my chest. It was so damn hard to believe that a kid of only twelve years could be so much smarter than someone almost three times her age.

"You have such a beautiful heart," I said. "I'm so scared it will be hurt again."

She pulled back and wiped her eyes with the palms of her hands. "I am too but you'll be there to comfort me if it happens again."

"Always."

"Maia?"

I lifted my head and Maia turned around. Kim was standing a few feet away from us, shifting from one foot to the other and fidgeting with her fingers. "I'm sorry I just showed up. I thought it would be okay."

My first instinct was to glower at this woman who had absolutely nothing to deserve the love and devotion of her daughter. But one look at Maia and I knew I couldn't do that. If I kept them apart, I would be robbing her of so much.

The best thing I could do for her was to step back and show her I trusted her judgment and if—heaven forbid—the worst happened, I would be there to pick up the pieces of her broken heart.

Kim's eyes bounced from Maia to me then settled on Maia again. Holding her arms open, she softly asked, "Can I…can I hug you?"

My heart almost gave out when instead of answering, Maia turned her questioning gaze to me. I stepped forward and pressed my lips against the top of her head. "You do what you gotta do."

"Love you, Dad."

I swallowed down the thick lump stuck in my throat as I watched Maia cautiously walk to Kim. The moment mother and daughter were locked in an embrace, Kim's entire body shook with the force of her tears.

I waited until they broke apart before joining them. And even though it felt awkward as hell, I smiled and listened as Kim told us she was in Clearwater Bay for the next five days. I even invited her out for dinner and agreed that she could spend time with Maia after school.

By the time we walked into the house a few hours later, I was completely exhausted, but my kid was happy. So damn happy. I'd listened to her while she told Kim how much she loved the beach and baking. I'd seen her shine while Kim thumbed through her drawings and praised her remarkable talent.

Yeah, my heart was pretty full save for that one spot that kept scratching. I needed to see Frankie. Needed to apologize for being an asshole. Because as I sat there and listened to Maia and Kim talk, I realized Frankie had been thinking about Maia when she stepped in to take the blame.

But it was late so my apology would have to wait until morning. Sure, I could call or text but I wanted to do this in person. Face to face so I could look into her eyes when I told her how much she meant to me.

"What a day," I muttered. Throwing my head back, I rolled it from side to side, almost groaning when a satisfying crunch rang through the air. I was about to head upstairs when a knock on the front door sounded.

Who the hell would be knocking on my door at this time in the evening? The thought barely formed when I remembered the night Frankie had come over. The night we shared our second first kiss.

Spinning on my heel, I rushed to the door and swung it open.

"What are you doing here?"

Caden pressed his hand to his chest. "Ouch. Not the greeting I was expecting."

"It's almost 9 PM."

"I called uncle Caden." I looked behind me to where Maia was standing. She must've seen the question on my face because she went on to explain, "I asked him to stay with me while you're gone."

"But I'm not going anywhere."

Caden pushed past me to walk into the house. Paying no attention to the conversation between me and Maia, he headed to the living room where he plopped down on the couch and switched the TV to some sports channel.

"Yes, you are," Maia said. "You need to apologize to Frankie."

I blew out a breath. She was right. I'd been thinking about it all day and deep down in my heart, I knew she did what she thought was right for Maia. It was the only thing that made sense.

"I don't want us to lose Frankie over some stupid misunderstanding, Dad."

"You should listen to your daughter, she's pretty smart," Caden piped up.

My gaze flicked between the two of them before I shrugged my shoulders and muttered, "I guess I'm leaving then."

Maia gave me an approving nod and then joined Caden in the living room. I stood there watching her for a few moments, completely stunned at the wonder that was my daughter. The way her brain so delicately and wisely put things together was so utterly amazing and I just hoped I had it within me to keep nurturing that.

Because the world needed more Maias.

"You're staring, Dad. It's weird."

A chuckle rumbled its way through my chest. "Alright, alright. I'm going." Shaking my head, I grabbed my keys and headed for the door. Since I wasn't expecting it, I hissed out a curse when I swung it open only to find Frankie standing on the other side with her hand awkwardly in the air.

"Hi." Lowering her hand, she shifted from one foot to the other.

I closed the door behind me. "I was actually on my way to see you." Placing my hand on her back, I guided her to the steps where we both sat down on the top one. "Maia told me the truth."

"I'm so—"

With a shake of my head, I pressed my fingers against her lips. "I'm the one who needs to apologize. I shouldn't have talked to you like that."

"And I shouldn't have kept the truth from you. I was just worried about Maia and I really didn't want her to get hurt."

Hooking my fingers behind her neck, I pulled her face to mine. With our foreheads touching and lips barely a whisper apart, I confessed, "I love the way you care about my daughter. I love how you enrich our lives. I just love *you*, Francesca Baker. So fucking much that some days I don't even know what to do with it all."

Frankie pulled back and cupped my cheeks between her palms. Those gorgeous blue eyes I just wanted to get lost in searching mine for what felt like an eternity. One corner of her mouth lifted right before she knocked the breath from my lungs.

"I love you too. Both of you."

My mouth was on hers not even a second later, my kiss hungry as I dipped my tongue between her lips to get that first taste of her. I wanted to savor the moment, to always remember how sweet those four words tasted.

And how Frankie melted into me.

Her arms wound around my neck, pulling me closer. My hands found her hips and just as I was about to lift her onto my lap, someone very obnoxiously cleared their throat behind us.

"Not that I'm a prude or anything but you sucking on my sister's face is an image I'd rather not see."

Reluctantly tearing my mouth away from Frankie's, I glared at her idiot brother. "No one told you to come outside, jackass. Now go away so I continue with my face sucking."

"Yeah, what he said." Frankie giggled and rested her head on my shoulder.

Caden pulled a face. "Oh joy, so this is what family dinners are going to look like from now on."

He was still talking when Maia poked her head out from behind him. The moment her eyes landed on Frankie, her face lit up and she rushed toward us. Plopping down, she threw her arms around Frankie who hugged her right back.

Tilting my head back, I looked at the night sky and smiled. My family was finally complete.

EPILOGUE

GAGE

"Is she orgasming regularly?"

Instead of going down, my beer came back up my throat and sputtered out of my mouth. "What the hell, Nan?"

"It's important, you know?" Nan pushed a teal tendril behind her ear. "You can buy a woman all sorts of gifts but the only way to keep her really happy is to make sure she has lots and lots of orgasms. If you're struggling, I can always ask Paul to give you a few pointers."

Paul was Nan's new boyfriend. Yup, my Nan had gotten herself a boyfriend at the age of (age) and she was making no secret of the fact that they liked to get frisky, much to everyone else's dismay.

They'd met when Nan moved to an old age home after she recovered from her hip surgery six months ago. Because she had been living alone, she was afraid she might fall and hurt herself again.

And no matter how many times Frankie and I had begged to her move in with us, she flat out refused. If you ask her now she'd say it was the best thing she could have done because it led her to Paul.

"We're heading out." Adam poked his head into the kitchen. "Maddie's just about ready for bed."

At the mention of her name, she stepped out behind Adam and rubbed her hands over her heavily pregnant belly. "I don't know what he's doing in there but it's exhausting."

Adam smiled and kissed the top of her head. To me he said, "See you tomorrow night."

"Sure thing, chief."

A lot had changed over the last six months. I took the job at the fire station and even though I wasn't getting as hands-on as I used to, I still owned half of Blue Ladder Construction. Caden and I just decided to bring in a few extra sets of hands.

Frankie's bakery was bigger and better than before and that was saying a lot considering how popular she'd been before the fire.

The biggest change was probably Maia's mom. She completed her program in Los Angeles and after getting a sponsor and a job she moved to Clearwater Bay to be closer to Maia. I admired the hell out of her for finally stepping up and being there for her daughter.

And Maia?

Well, she thrived. The more time she spent with Frankie the more she came out of her shell. It wasn't long before she opened up at school and finally made some friends. She'd even joined an art program over summer break.

Most days, I still had to pinch myself into believing that this was my life now.

"We should probably go too," Nan said. "Walk me to the door?"

I held out my arm, and she hooked her hand around my elbow. "Seeing you like this makes me so happy, Gage. This little slice of heaven was all I ever wanted for you."

"Thank you, Nan." I placed my hand on hers.

"So proud of you."

Frankie fell into step next to Nan. "I was just looking for you. Paul is already waiting outside."

When we reached the door Nan pulled me into a hug and whisper-shouted, "Just let me know if you need those pointers." After giving both me and Frankie a kiss, she slowly made her way to where Paul was waiting by the car.

He kissed her on the cheek then opened the passenger side door. Once she was in, he turned and waved to us before making his way to the driver's side.

"What was that about?"

Putting my arm around her waist, I tugged her close to me as we watched them drive away. They were the last of our dinner guests to leave and I couldn't be happier. Not that I didn't enjoy spending time with all the people in our circle, I was just anxious to have Frankie all to myself.

"Nan seems to think the only way to make a woman happy is by giving her orgasms." I let my eyes slowly drift down the length of her body before meeting her gaze again. "Lots of them apparently."

"Mmm, smart woman your Nan."

Tucking my fingers under her chin, she tilted her head back and lowered my mouth to hers in a soft kiss. "I better get started then. Wouldn't want my woman to be unhappy."

"Oh no, we can't have that." Slipping her fingers into my hair, she pulled my mouth back to hers.

"Ew!" Maia groaned. "Can you wait until I'm in bed before doing that or at least close the front door, I'm pretty sure Mrs. Hebert from across the street doesn't want to see that either."

I threw my head back and laughed. I swear the moment this kid turned thirteen she became a teenager in every sense of the word. Pretty sure I was sporting a few gray hairs with her name on them too.

"Did you come down here just to give us grief? I walked over to where she was standing and ruffled her hair. "Or did you want something?"

"Stop it." Maia smacked my hand away. "I came to say good night." Then she went to Frankie and hugged her. It didn't matter how many times I'd seen it, my heart always turned over at the sight of them together.

After she and Frankie shared a few whispered words, it was my turn to get a hug from my daughter. "Have a good sleep. Love you, Maia."

"Love you too, Dad."

I was still watching her make her way up the stairs when Frankie sidled in beside me. "Maybe it's bedtime for us too?" She didn't give me time to respond simply went about locking the doors before taking my hand and dragging my ass to our bedroom.

The door barely clicked shut before I had her pinned against it. "Now where were we?" I moved in for a kiss but Frankie ducked out of the way before our lips touched. I was about to protest when she slowly dropped to her knees.

Peering up at me from those impossibly thick lashes, her mouth stretched into a wide smile. She moved fast, undoing my pants and dragging them down my legs.

Her fingers hot as she tightly wrapped them around my cock.

One last smile was all she gave me before bent forward and sucked me into her mouth. "Holy shit!" I hissed.

Bracing one hand on the door, I looked down. My world almost exploded at the sight of her hot little mouth moving over me. And don't even get me started on how damn good it felt.

"Touch yourself." I ground out

Without a single ounce of hesitation, she reached under her dress, a moan vibrating around my cock not even a second later.

"Are you wet for me?"

Without taking her mouth off me, Frankie bobbed her head as much as she could.

"Show me."

Those blue eyes flicked to mine as she slowly pulled her hand out from under her dress and lifted her fingers toward me. They glistened. In one swift motion, I gripped her wrist and bent forward so I could pull her fingers into my mouth.

I needed more though. I always did when it came to this woman.

Hooking my hands under her arms, I yanked her up and immediately pressed my mouth to hers. Slipping my tongue through the seam of her lips, I coiled it around hers and savored the taste of us.

Stepping out of my pants, I lifted her and carried her to the bed. After stripping off the rest of our clothes, Frankie fell back against the sheets with me hovering over her.

“You’re so beautiful,” I said as I brushed my fingertips up her thigh and over her hip bone. “And you’re mine.” I continued to trace a path up her stomach around her breast and along her collarbone.

Lowering my face to hers, I sealed my mouth over hers and settled between her thighs. “I love you,” I whispered against her lips just as I pushed into her.

ALSO BY A.K. MACBRIDE

ALL BOOKS ARE FREE IN KINDLE UNLIMITED

Willow Creek:
Shattered
Wrecked
Ruined

Breathing Hearts:
Instant Heat
Slow Burn)

Cocky Hero Club:
Egotistical Jerk

Montana Dudes:
Broken Roads

Standalone Titles:
An Inconvenient Marriage

Novellas:
Stuck on you
The Other Brother

Please visisit www.akmacbride.com for more information.